I0573629

The Nature of Things

Ellen Wilson

Chapter 1

I remember sitting in the truck and looking out on the valley. Morning light had just begun to filter through the forest; drifts of fog hung heavy in the treetops and clung to the shallows among the hills. It was peaceful, and I felt totally present; feeling the movement of my breath as I watched the trees sway in a slight breeze, dissipating the fog into the emerging light. I rested my head on the seat and closed my eyes.

A call sliced through the emptiness, and I jumped. I quickly picked up; listened, then spoke, not remembering what I had said a second before. I watched myself as if far away; becoming acutely aware that a fearful dream had begun to unwind, and there was nothing for me to do but to play it out. The air had become heavy and the crickets chirping along with it, the sound reverberating in the air as my heart began racing.

Falling into fear, I stepped on the gas and clenched the steering wheel, barely keeping the truck on the road as tires skittered through gravel. My hands became wet and I quickly wiped them on my pants. Speeding towards the lake the ancient white pines flicked through my line of vision; blue water, then the red bait shop sign flashed by and the campground rolled into sight.

Turning into the drive I saw people clustered around a police car. Patrol lights splashed their frozen faces in a kaleidoscope of color.

I threw the gear in park and jumped out.

"What happened?"

Officer Kepola turned to me, his face strained. "The bear got into the girls tent sometime in the early morning. Damn thing started eating her here, in the abdomen," He put a protective hand to his beer belly. "then started in on her buttocks. I didn't find it. Didn't get here in time. Poor girl is lucky to be alive." He shook his head.

I looked over to where the paramedics were loading the girl into the ambulance. There was blood everywhere. I could smell the tang of it. She looked unconscious, head rolling off to the side. I hoped for her sake she was.

I blamed Dale for this. For all of this. She knew better. She had been through the training—animals are not human, do not get attached to them, develop any type of relationship with them. Simply observe and leave them be.

But she had grown fond of the bears in her assigned territory, naming them even. She smiled when she told me of their antics, how cute they were, she said, how sweet.

I had clenched my jaw when I listened to her rambling, explained to her how black bear were opportunists, not Disney creatures, when they came across something they could kill easily, they would, a newborn fawn for instance. Kill it then cache it for later. She had merely shrugged and pretended not to hear, content with her fuzzy wuzzy bear fantasy.

Then a bear had been spotted in the campground, hanging around, taking handouts. I told her to get rid of the animal. And waited.

She hadn't always been so soft. So saccharine.

"So it's out there somewhere?" My eyes scanned the trees.

He nodded. "They could hardly get it off her when she was screaming. Snarled at them, tried to drag her out of the tent. Course by that time she was passed out from shock."

"Have you talked to any of these people?"

He motioned towards a man and a woman. "Those are the parents. And the guys over there were kind enough to give me the gruesome details," Slight shake of the head towards a guy with a blue bandana and another with a leather vest. "Sure the parents appreciated that."

I followed his eyes over to where they sat lounging in front of a fire.

"Hey man, why didn't you warn us?" Bandana man had stepped forward when he caught me watching him. He turned towards Kepola. "People here are saying this thing has been wandering around the campground harassing people all summer."

"Look, I don't control the campground, that's the park service's job. They are in charge of observing and controlling nuisance wildlife," Kepola pushed the stray hair out of his eyes.

The woman looked over. Her face was pale and her eyes red. Shaking, she rubbed her nose on the sleeve of her blue windbreaker, leaving a wet streak on the arm.

"Is that true, should we have been warned about this animal?" Are you in charge here?" She stared at me.

"The bear was to removed far from human contact. Unfortunately, we hadn't been able to trap the bear to remove it."

The man stepped forward, standing protectively by the woman's side. "You didn't answer my wife's question, should we have been warned?"

"Wild animals are unpredictable, if you need a warning you shouldn't go outside."

The woman gasped. "I hardly think that's the attitude..." Shaking her head, she put her hand to her mouth and walked away. My eyes followed her to a large, square shaped RV. She opened the door and went inside.

He watched the woman enter the RV, then turned to me. "My wife's in a lot of pain and you treat us like this. I don't need this shit from a park worker."

"I work for wildlife division sir."

"Who is in charge here?" His eyes shot from Kepola to me again.

Kepola looked at him. "Whoever is first to respond to the call is in charge."

"So you mean to tell me that no one is responsible for what happened today? No one is in charge here?"

I watched his face change expression—eyes distant, face furrowed with bitterness, full of anger, then hate. I had seen it before in victims of accidents; looking for someone, or something to blame.

"I'm in charge of wildlife management in this area."

"Now the truth comes out.'

"I'm writing up my report, Clare. You got this under control?"

"Yeah. Thanks Sam." Kepola walked over to his patrol car.

I studied the man a moment. His face was tan, windblown. He looked like he had been on a boat all summer, or on a golf course Probably one of the upper crusts from Chicago, I thought absently, or the suburbs of Detroit.

"Like I mentioned, sir, wild animals can be unpredictable."

"But is it true what people have been saying about the bear harassing people?"

"What's true is that people have been feeding the bear, and yes, we've known about it. There are warnings posted all over the campground about not feeding the bears."

"Your piddly warnings didn't help us. They don't mention how dangerous this animal is."

I was silent a moment then walked over to a utility pole, ripped off a notice and read from it: "A fed bear is a dangerous bear. Here."

He looked at me; my arm outstretched, holding the notice. "That's not what I'm talking about."

"That's what I'm talking about. And that's what happened."

"My daughter did not feed that animal, she was in her tent!"

"It doesn't matter. The bear equated humans with food."

He stared at the woods in front of us. The sun had risen past tree line and the hemlock and pine were now in shadow. I suddenly realized how tired I was.

He pointed an accusing finger at me. "I'm suing the park service. And you and whoever you work for." He glared at me; walked away.

I watched him a moment, wondering if I should say something, something to explain this awful mess, when a spiteful little laugh erupted behind me. I turned and saw that the bandana guy was sitting on a log watching me, smirking. His leathered companion sat next to him with a beer in his hand.

"You are one *mean* lady. Don't you have any compassion? Bandana guy cocked his head and narrowed his eyes, blowing smoke in my direction. I opened my mouth to respond; thought better of it. I turned away from him and walked back to my truck, got in and drove away.

Chapter 2

Pheeny Delmato did not like deadlines. Her once empty and neatly organized desk was now occupied with either a new case or information relating to an existing case. Sighing, she picked up a document.

Footsteps clicked outside her door.

 "Hey Christine!"

Christine opened the door, timidly sticking her head in.

"Yes, Ms. Delmato?"

"Could you please get us some lunch? Maybe at Dewey's? I have to get this deposition done by tomorrow. I'd really appreciate it."

Christine nodded.

"I was thinking maybe a sub," Pheeny opened a drawer, extracting her purse. "Here's a twenty."

Christine gingerly plucked the bill from Pheeny's fingers.

"Sure thing Ms Delmato, right after I finish this filing."

"I'll have the usual pastrami, extra Italian dressing."

After she said it she wished she would have chosen differently. She always chose the same thing. She feared she was getting too rigid, too set in her ways. Maybe a new choice would help her to view this case from a different angle.

"Oh, but get me one of those sumptuous brownies with nuts. You can't be good all the time." Pheeny patted her waistline.

She looked at Christine a moment. "So I hear you're expecting. You don't look like it. Guess you can eat what you want, huh?"

Christine laughed. "Gosh, I'm only a few months. Word travels fast around here."

Pheeny yawned, and interlacing her fingers, she raised her hands over her head and tried to stretch the knot between her shoulders out.

"Yeah it does, gossip mill that it is around here. So what does it feel like?"

"I have a few cramps. Feel kind of tired. That's about it."

"That's it huh?"

"That's it."

"It doesn't hurt?"

She laughed again. "No, that doesn't come until labor." She smiled, looked down at the floor.

"Well I better get going. Get this done."

"Oh. Okay."

Christine quietly closed the door.

Pheeny again turned to the file before her, a suspect bio of Wilfred Durant. He was the largest developer in the Midwest; famous for buying up large tracks of prime vacation land, lakeshore properties, or old farms nestled in national forests. Known as durable Durant in the business, he had an uncanny knack for waiting out properties, usually old farms. Making little profit on their land, farmers would often be desperate to sell. Caught between a rock and a hard place and holding out as long as they could, they contemplated local and state monies to save their land against the large dollars of the developers. Who could refuse? And Durant was usually there holding the largest bill of all.

She remembered Joe talking about developers buying up land, habitat degradation he had called it. He talked about it in terms of wildlife running out of places to live.

She stared at a distant point along the Chicago skyline, thinking of all that money. How money could buy innocence.

The crime photo of Dee Dee Banks haunted her. A black and white picture embedded in her thoughts. During her tired days, the old memory record would skip across to the injured groove, playing again and again. She lay face down in a pool of blood and her hands had been bound at the wrist, lopped off, then discarded. Never to be found.

Pheeny had consulted a criminal psychologist about the mutilation. It disturbed her, she had never come across anything so sadistic. She wanted to understand a personality that would do this. He said that you fashion a life from the hands, and to cut them off was a very personal thing. Look for someone close to the victim, he told her, someone with sexual problems.

And what about Kyle Banks? Dee Dee was a single mom. The child stared at her from her mind's eye. She had made some calls to social services but had gotten nowhere. The usual run-a-round.

"Ms Delmato?" Christine knocked on the door. "I'm leaving to get our lunch."

"Hey Christine, come in a second." Pheeny looked up from the file as Christine entered. "Please…call me Josephine. Do you want to go to lunch together? I'd sure love to get out of this office for a while."

"Well sssure," Christine stammered, blushing. "I'd like that very much."

"All right then, lunch it is." Pheeny smiled.

Chapter 3

The morning air was crisp, you could sense it in the stillness of the trees. We were making our way to the tribal school; it was on the outskirts of town, on the reservation. The road started to curve and circled up a hill, giving way to a wide, valley view of pine and yellow tamarack. We drove in silence for a long time. I was content in the passenger seat gazing out the window. The sky was a brilliant blue and a rich light spilled through the trees, dappling the road in gold. I thought of apples. Finally, I glanced over at Darla. Her face was pinched, but that wasn't surprising. She had been nervous and jumpy since she had gotten the administrative position over at the school.

It was an Indian school, the first of its kind on the reservation. Everyone was eager to make it work, a school completely controlled by the Tribe. A school devoted to Indian values. But it looked like they were going to have to close it down after only a year due to financial and personnel problems. In desperation they contacted Darla, she had a MS in school administration. She had been working downstate on educational programs for Indians living outside of the reservation.

"Now promise me you won't slip in any state versus tribal things, those sticky resource issues," She started picking lint off her red blazer.

I watched her a moment, taking in her outfit. "Darla, did you dress to match your Bronco on purpose?

I've noticed you've been taking this organizational thing to an extreme."

"Clare! Quit picking on me. Just promise." She adjusted her glasses.

"All right. I promise,"

I looked out the window at a passing field dotted with dead stalks of black-eyed Susans. I thought of the isolation here—fifty miles between towns, a handful of cabins between. The road stretched like a long finger through the wilderness.

"Dale got the ax, did I tell you? I suppose they had to fire her because they were looking to blame somebody."

"Yeah. Just like the government. Yours that is," She looked over at me. "Well, if I recall you said yourself it was her fault."

"That's true, but I didn't think she should have been fired for it. She was going to get rid of the bear. I told her to."

Darla raised her eyebrows.

"Well, I did. I am the boss."

"Yeah? So everyone jumps when you tell them to?" She made a face, sticking her tongue out at me.

I crossed my arms in front of me and frowned. She was the only friend I had here up here.

Crossing the bridge over the water, I had left the mitten state of Michigan for a precarious piece of land known as the Upper Peninsula. I was in another world. Time moved slowly here, it was a place of the past. People up here called themselves Yoopers, were proud to be disconnected from the rest of the state; had at one point even tried to secede from it by becoming a separate state.

I rested my head on the seat and stared out at the trees rushing by.

Darla was looking at me from her place at the steering wheel. "Clare, I guess I don't care if you talk about Tribe versus state issues, it's just how they're stated that's important. I don't want these kids getting polarized in their thinking," She rubbed her nose, thinking. The nose rub was something she always did when there was friction in the conversation. "It's more important now than ever that we keep the lines of communication open."

"I know that." I was irritated that she would insinuate I might say something inappropriate regarding fishing rights.

There had been a long standing conflict over how the state and the Tribe viewed the 1836 treaty. The Tribe saw the treaty as a moment in time, this was the one binding agreement between whites and the Tribe—it must be adhered to. The state viewed the agreement a little differently, it was felt the situation was much more fluid, treaties could be changed in regards to the resource.

"Don't worry Darla. We can always chat about something a little more innocuous; how about predator prey relationships? Black bear munching on humans for instance."

"Yeah, right Clare. Very funny."

***

I had just finished my talk on forest ecosystems and nutrient cycling. I prided myself on how well this was going, the kids were attentive and politely asked questions. Moving now into population dynamics, I drew a fish on the blackboard, hoping it resembled a salmon. I stepped back to admire my work.

"Miss McElroy, why is it we ran out of fish when the white man came?"

I turned around, contemplated the kid who just had to be smart ass of the day. Roddy Shagonaby, a small kid sitting in the front row. He looked about thirteen and his brown eyes snapped at me. I knew his uncle was a tribal fisherman.

I took a deep breath. "The fishery resource has really taken a beating due to over harvesting from various sources. What it boils down to is too many people, too little fish."

"You mean too many white people."

"Let's not give our special lecturer a beating," said Darla. "She has come here to discuss nature and the various ecosystems, not tribal politics over fish harvesting." She nervously pushed her glasses back along the bridge of her nose.

"Yeah well, I don't know what a white woman from the city knows 'bout anything here." Roddy mumbled loud enough for the other boys around to get a good laugh.

I felt my face turn hot, heating up to a bright crimson. "Look Roddy, I know your uncle is constantly harassed by fishermen. Now is not the time or place to take this up. Got it?" I was surprised at the anger that welled up in me, at the words barked out of my mouth. The kids stared at me wide eyed. There was an embarrassing silence, then Darla cleared her throat.

"All right class, let's rap this up and give Ms. McElroy a hand for coming." She feebly started clapping for me. No one else bothered to join in.

***

The late afternoon sun fell on a stand of conifers as we rounded a turn in the road.

We passed a few ramshackled farmsteads with corn shocks and pumpkins in front of the houses. Not much farming in the Upper Peninsula, days too short, and temperatures too cold.

Darla turned left and a deer darted in front of us.

"Damn it!" She jerked the steering wheel to avoid it. The deer bounded off the road into a thicket of trees.

I looked over at her. "So are you going to talk now? Or is that the extent of the conversation coming home?"

She glanced over, then straight ahead again, setting her mouth in a firm line.

"You know Clare, I was hoping today would go a little smoother."

"Smoother?"

She bent over and pushed the cigarette lighter down in the Bronco console.

"Hey, I thought you were off that crappy habit."

"Hey, well I'm not." She held the lighter to her cigarette, took a long drag, and exhaled. "You had to go and draw a fish on the board."

"Oh c'mon, so what?"

"Fishing Clare? So what?" She flicked her cigarette ashes in the console ashtray. "You could have just as well drew anything else, a beaver, badger, anything else but that."

"Now you're going to critique my teaching ability?"

"Don't play dumb with me, I warned you about this."

"Warned me? It was a fish Darla, a salmon, granted it didn't look like one but it was a picture and had nothing to do with Indian fishing rights. If that hothead kid saw more in it than I intended, well, that's his problem not mine. I will not go around walking on eggshells. That's ridiculous."

Darla was silent a moment, rubbing her nose. "You'll never understand what it's like Clare, never. Look at this, all of this," She waved her hand around, indicating the land before us. "Now we have imposed boundaries; we have a reservation."

"What's that got to do with fishing?"

"Another imposed boundary."

"There's nothing I can do about that. I'm just one person, in the here and now."

"Yeah, but we can make a difference in the here and now, make things more fair, more just. Teach people the truth."

We lapsed into silence. I rolled up the window and turned the radio on. Static. I turned it off. The Bronco hit a pot hole, we bounced, then leveled out.

"This whole fishing thing is getting way out of hand. It scares the hell out of me that it could get very volatile, very quickly. Remember what happened in Wisconsin with those spear fishermen?"

I nodded. "I remember."

"Anyway," She glanced over, a tired expression on her face. "Let's go have a beer."

The parking lot at Moe's tavern was full when we pulled up. I pulled along the side, parked in the grass. Hunter orange was everywhere. It was the beginning of rifle season for deer.

We crossed over the antler threshold and entered the bar. The air hung heavy with smoke, the smell of tapped beer, and tall tales of hunter heroics. Conversation was jostled back and forth as men stood everywhere: boot to boot, cap to cap. Darla and I stood mashed together in the middle of the aisle next to the bar. Peanut shells crunched under our feet as more shells were chucked and tossed below tables and chairs. Moe had started the peanut tradition when he opened the place twenty odd years ago. I felt a bing on the back of my head. A peanut.

I turned and spotted my neighbor, landlord really, sitting at the bar. I tugged Darla's arm and we started squeezing our way over. Darryl asked the guy next to him to kindly give up his chair.

"Clare, I need to talk to you 'bout somethin."

"I hope you have a ride home Darryl. Where's Kyle?"

"At his grandma's, and I'm fine to drive, thank you very much officer. Say, what am I gonna do about that tom turkey? He's back again with a vengeance, had to chase him off five times last night. Just when I thought I was rid of him," He paused, swigged his beer. "I'm about ready to eat him for dinner, put him out of his misery. Hey, Thanksgiving's right around the corner Clare. Problem solved." He slapped the table in good humor.

"I don't know Darryl. Maybe the turkey isn't miserable. And what about the deer teasing the horses? Between the deer and the turkey you have a veritable circus in your backyard."

It was true, the wildlife were putting on quite a show. The turkey had taken a disliking to his image in the basement window—he'd peck at it. If there was a full moon we could hear him pecking into the night. He was extremely persistent, returning right after we chased him away, night after night. His beak was even bloody on occasion. We figured he has some sort of moon madness, because turkeys are not nocturnal birds.

Then to top it all off, we had deer teasing the two horses at the break of dawn. We would hear the horses whinnying and racing up and down the field. I'd look out the window to see what was going on. The deer would be calmly chewing their cud, watching the horses making spectacles of themselves.

"I guess it's just the nature of things," I swigged down a mouthful of beer. "Animals are much smarter than we give them credit for. They've got their own agenda."

"Smart!" Darryl snorted. "You call a turkey pecking a piece of glass 'cuz he thinks it's another turkey is smart? I call it as dumb as they come."

"Hey Darryl," said Darla, "Just because animals have a different type of intelligence compared to humans doesn't make them dumb. It just makes them different from us. Since when does the human animal become the paradigm of intelligence that all other animals must be judged by?"

"What? What are you talking about?" Darryl looked confused. "Is that an Indian thing or what?"

"Damn right it's an Indian thing!" Darla kicked him under the bar.

"It is rather anthropomorphic, comparing animals to humans." I said.

"Anthropo what?" Now Darryl really looked confused. "I'm sorry but this dumb white boy can't keep up with you two. I'll see ya at home hon." Darryl threw down a five spot, gave the back of my neck a squeeze, then started inching his way past the crowd.

I watched incredulously as he worked his way through the mass of orange hunters. "Hon? Can you believe it?" I rubbed my neck.

"I can believe it. He likes you."

"Don't talk like that. I have to live next to him."

"It's true."

"Doesn't mean I have to like it."

Darla was massaging her temples. "I feel a nasty headache coming on. I think I'll take off, chase down Darryl and give him a ride. You coming?" She swigged down the last of her beer.

"No. I'd rather sit here and let Darryl get a head start."

"All right, see ya then. Hon." She laughed, glancing back at me as she jumped off her bar stool, long, dark ponytail swinging as she left.

Chapter 4

Joe Delmato scratched his head and read the report on his desk. The target species was black bear, *Ursus americanus*. Review and recommendations concerning target species were in order, resulting in a fine tuning of existing management plan. Of course all it really boiled down to was getting into the state's business and stepping on a few toes. He rolled his eyes, hearing the backlash now.

The report was written by a woman wildlife biologist concerning a bear attack. Scanning the document with little interest, his mind began to wander.

He gazed out the window at the high rises shielding the city, the metallic sheen made him blink. There's a certain futuristic appeal to this, he thought, good for abstraction. He wondered absently how many abstractions had been thought and analyzed while pondering the views of a city.

Forcing himself back to the report he read on. She had described the event as a human versus nature conflict, which was true enough. Normally bears avoided people, but if around humans enough, fed by humans enough, the situation grew dangerous.

The black bear was a far ranging species too, old males ranging as much over two hundred square miles from their homes. It was inevitable that that there would be human and bear conflicts. He could well imagine the needs of people and bears were a touchy subject amongst people up there. What people never seemed to get was there was a finite supply of natural resources and a seemingly infinite supply of humans.

Tapping his pencil on his desk he frowned, tried to focus on what was really bugging him.

He scanned the report again. Maybe it was the attitude of the woman who had wrote it that bothered him. Her tone was certainly condescending in respect to how people had viewed and experienced the incident. He thought of Pheeny, the endless rounds spent with her arguing a point. She always had to be right, would never lose an argument, or even concede one graciously, he thought irritably. And this woman seemed to be all brass and no polish, just like his sister.

Joe glanced at his watch and stood up, hurriedly putting documents in his briefcase. He had a plane to catch.

***

Chaos prevailed at Chicago O'Hare, people were coming and going from every direction. Joe sat stiffly in his chair, determined to remain calm. His 10:30 am flight had been cancelled. The woman behind the counter had calmly and matter of factly promised that a new flight would be scheduled within the hour. Probably. Joe gritted his teeth and refrained from snapping at her.

Every one of his nerves were set on edge. He comforted himself with the thought that his coffee buzz was wearing off and he soon would be on the verge of obtaining calm.

A woman in a beautifully colored sari wandered by. The sari was saffron and red with gold lame ribbon lining the garment. She had a crimson dot in the middle of her forehead and looked very serene. Serene enough to catch his eye in this place of bursting bustle. He wanted that serenity.

A well-dressed couple argued quietly and vehemently amongst themselves. The man was wearing a three piece suit, and the woman was dressed in a similar businesslike fashion, with a green tailored skirt and blazer. A little girl clutched the woman's hand; stared up at their faces.

Typical two working parent family probably, he thought, arguing about some knotted up problem in their lives.

That was the problem with knots, they took care to become undone.

He thought about the life that was no longer his. He had started his career working for the US Fish and Wildlife service. The field office was nestled in a remote wilderness area of the Upper Peninsula of Michigan called the Porcupine Mountains. Aptly named by the Native Americans, they were reminiscent of crouched porcupines leading to Lake Superior. True, the porkies were not real mountains, they fell forty feet shy of the geological definition, but Joe remembered his aching muscles after hiking up a strenuous trail. That was mountain enough for him.

The assignment had been a recovery plan for the bald eagle which was listed as an endangered species on the national register. He had driven many miles in the government truck collecting road kill to put on frozen lakes to feed the eagles. Juvenile eagles had a bad habit of gorging on road kill and subsequently slamming into moving vehicles when unable to get up the speed and momentum to clear the road. Just one of the hazards of being young. Biologists had hit on the bright idea of carcass collection when they analyzed this mortality factor.

The air was so clean there, the views so crisp. Joe breathed deeply in, remembering the aroma of lake air and damp woods: patchouli woods after a rain, with the sweet smell of cedar and earth.

The research area was on top of a high hill. Headquarters had a panoramic view of Lake Superior and miles of green topped trees. He chuckled to himself thinking of headquarters, a small cabin with enough bunks for ten team members, an old cook stove, and an ancient couch that was inhabited by mice. One of the team members had thrown a brightly colored rag rug down to give the cabin a homey touch.

They often sat for hours around the table, playing cards, joking, laughing. Marty would bring out cigars, and they would play poker, substituting smooth beach stones for poker chips. Who ever won for the night had a weeks worth of home cooked meals. The guys could get pretty creative with the fish and venison they brought in. The nearest town was fifty two miles away.

The assignment was to gather vital information on eagle reproduction and mortality. Every morning, two team members would search the surrounding area for an eagle aerie. Eagles would usually lay two to three eggs. One team member would scale a tree where a nest had been located and count the eggs. The nest location was carefully plotted on a map.

Joe scaled the trees. He enjoyed the physical strain it took to pull himself up a trunk. Marty would anxiously fret below.

"C'mon Delmato, mama eagle's gonna be here soon!"

"Yeah, yeah. I'm coming."

With sharp beaks and plunging talons, eagles go to great lengths to protect their young. Joe would quickly count the eggs and plot the nest on the map.

He would often sit alone on top of a rocky hill, watching the valley and the lake below, the sunrise spilling pink and gold across the sky. A pileated woodpecker had once startled him; as he walked along a ridge it flew from a tree, screaming. On the wings of the woodpecker he heard a great whoosh. Looking up, he saw that not more than fifteen feet above him flew an adult eagle. It caught his eye, burning through him and becoming one with all things as it flew over the valley. Transforming into a mere spec in the sky, he followed it as long as he could, his eyes blinking it in and out of existence.

Joe understood the Native American reverence for the eagle, a bird that flew higher than any other. Once a month a tribal elder would come to collect the eagle feathers. It was illegal for people other than Indians to possess them and he willingly handed them over.

So it went day after day for five years. Then the project was over and the bald eagle was taken off the endangered species list.

All in the wink of an eye.

The higher-ups decided to promote him. They moved him all the way to headquarters in Chicago, added a big bonus to his check every year and promised that his field days weren't over. He would just have a few more desk duties. That's all.

Well, a few desk duties had turned into a regulatory nightmare. Constant paper pushing.

Joe's thoughts turned to Clare McElroy and how he was going to approach this problem. He really hated messing with the state's business, but there was no way around it. The feds had the authority to review and change management plans on state owned land if natural resources personnel had a major problem. And a black bear munching on a person constituted a major problem.

Ms. McElroy knew he was coming and he hoped there wouldn't be much fanfare. He had investigated a case similar to this where a mountain lion was stalking cross country skiers in the northern reaches of Minnesota. The story had wound up in all the state papers as well as the national nightly news. "Flight 409 boarding at gate E, flight 409, Chicago to Marquette, boarding."

Joe walked through the terminal and handed the flight attendant his ticket.

"Thank you sir, have a good flight." She smiled at him. Her name tag read Denise.

Joe smiled back at Denise, even though he wasn't feeling very happy. He hated flying.

***

When he arrived at his hotel the late afternoon sun was hitting Keeweenaw Bay, turning the water a molten gold. From his room window he tried to imagine what it would look like without all the lumber and earth piles from recent excavation. They detracted from the view of the bay and surrounding forest.

The Tribe had recently built this casino and hotel, it was a guaranteed money maker. Bus loads of old folks came in daily from down state, he could see the tour buses parked out front. He could never figure out what the attraction was pulling down the handle of a slot machine, quarter after quarter, glassy eyed and tense. Always waiting for that win.

Still, it was a nice place. Nice big bed, firm too. Everything was brand new. There was even a jacuzzi in the corner. The paintings on the walls looked like they were painted by Natives. Joe walked over and examined an abstract print of loons and rushes. It was signed by a Lestor Kishigo. He felt reassured by the signature; the print wasn't made in China. Maybe the Tribe hadn't forgotten its roots.

He sat on the edge of his bed and looked out the window, watching as people exited from a bus in the

23

parking lot, entering the hotel with racks of shirts and rolled suitcases. Probably up for a weekend of gambling, he thought absently.

He was not looking forward to meeting with Ms McElroy. He felt prepared, federal regulation made sure of that. Everything had been ironed out, papers were in order and thoroughly wrinkle free. It bothered him the way bureaucracy could reduce nature to a document.

Joe looked over at the dresser for his room key. Grabbing it, he headed out the door.

***

After driving for a while he had discovered the bar along the water. An old log cabin with a wooden porch out front. The red sign simply announced 'Moe's' in black letters. Deer antlers hung above the door threshold, and when he entered the bar it was dark and smelled of smoke. Two windows on either side of a row of booths faced the parking lot, filtering in a weak light.

He finished a hamburger and chewed on the straw of his rum and Coke, taking in the bar. Two guys were at the pool table playing a round of eightball. By the sound of it it appeared like they had been here a while—quarters flushing in, balls rolling out—all on a pretty rhythmic basis. A couple sat on the other side of the bar looking like they had had one too many three hours ago.

"Hey mistah, where ya from?" The woman bobbed her head in his direction, drunken eyes trying to grab hold of him.

Joe eyed her levelly, this wasn't the type of person he wanted to have a conversation with.

"Roxy, that's enough. You two have had your quota for the day." Moe glanced in their direction as he gave the shot glasses a vigorous rub down.

"Aw, Moe babe, one more round. *Puhleeze...*" She swayed her drunken eyes over to him, tried to look seductive.

"That's it. Out. You heard me. Now leave before I bar you from coming back for good."

Knowing he meant business, the woman and her companion grumbled under their breath as they stumbled off their barstools. They propped each other up as they weaved their way out of the bar. Light flooded the room from the open door, making Joe wince. Then the door slammed shut, leaving him with Moe's dark figure standing in front of him. The figure slowly started to materialize.

"Sorry 'bout that. This job leaves you with all kinds. Especially that kind," Moe nodded his head in the direction of the door. "The sad thing is, it's not just her life, she's got two little ones at home. God knows where they're at this instant. Every other day I'm kicking her out, her and some guy. You learn about human nature here. Here behind this bar."

"Yeah. I bet," Joe finished his drink and sat it on the bar. He resumed chewing on his straw then stopped. "I suppose it would get to you, depressing situations like that."

"Oh damn right, you're not kidding. But I try to stay upbeat about it ya know, I try to learn from people, and sometimes I even wind up doing some good, helping them ya know. That's why I'm taking this class over at the college. I aim to get my degree in psychology."

Moe reached under the bar and pulled out a large book. A heavy volume, Joe recognized it as some sort of textbook. The cover was blue and green with pictures of people involved in various communicative situations; a mother holding a little boy, a teacher lecturing a class. The title read: *The Human Condition – Psychological Dimensions of Personality.* He displayed the book to Joe, then thought better of it. Embarrassed, Moe quickly placed the book under the bar.

"You seem like a level kind of guy, someone who has some education."

"I have a little education. A college degree."

Moe lined the next shot glass up next to the last on the bar with purpose and precision. He grabbed another from the sink and again began to rub vigorously.

"See, right off I recognized you as a smart guy, someone who knows about people." He smiled contentedly to himself.

"Actually, I don't work much with people. Well I do, but that's only secondary to what I really do."

Moe looked up quizzically. "Yeah? What do you really do?"

"I'm a wildlife biologist."

"Oh." Moe went back to polishing glasses, setting another on the bar. He looked up suddenly, "I got it. You're that guy come to talk to Ms. McElroy. The bear thing," Moe looked at Joe, a serious expression on his face. "Everyone's been on pins and needles about that, especially Ms. McElroy. Her name is Clare ya know, but I think she likes it when I call her that. She deserves that respect."

He placed the last glass in the row and put his elbows on the bar. A card from a Vegas nightclub was wedged between the glass and the rippley water stained wood of the bar. Joe studied the card, The Sands Nightclub. The card had an Elvis signature in the lower right-hand corner. Joe thought it was a strange card to have in an Upper Peninsula bar. But then he remembered the casinos.

"Well, this is official business, I can't really talk about the case with you…sorry, I don't know your name."

"Moe. Moe Hansen," He stuck his beefy arm out for a handshake. "Please to meet you."

Joe extended his hand and had it vigorously shaken. The guy's obviously doing something besides reading psyche textbooks by the strength of that handshake, he thought. There was a faint smell of grilled onions as he let go of Moe's hand.

"Well anyways," Moe continued, "We all think mighty highly of Ms. McElroy around here. The ones that don't have some kind of hunting violation anyways. She has worked really hard around here, educating the kids and all. That's important, don't you think? All them people in government keep on telling us it's the next generation that counts. The way I see it, we have someone here to help with that, she really protects things around here." Moe stopped, pleased with himself and his representation of Clare.

"Certainly that's nice to know. I'm glad everyone thinks so highly of Ms. McElroy." Joe glanced towards the guys playing pool. He wondered if these two thought highly of Ms. McElroy. They each had vapid expressions.

"And Dale, that other biologist. I think she meant well. You just can't get attached to the critters, they're not zoo animals for God's sake. Ms. McElroy knows that for sure, but maybe they don't teach that at the academy?" Moe scrutinized Joe for his opinion.

Joe surveyed the bar top again, finding a picture of a snowy owl, then a picture of people madly racing in their snowmobiles. He didn't know how to respond to that question. Getting into a philosophical discussion of people's perceptions of wildlife could be tricky. He didn't know if he really wanted to take the plunge.

"Certainly as professionals we are taught to be objective," he said. "But ultimately it's up to the individual to process that info—"

The door burst open, spilling into the premises three guys eager and red faced.

"Hey Moe, set us up with a couple of drafts."

"Sure Bill." He turned from Joe, busying himself with his new customers.

Joe lay his money down and quietly left the bar.

Chapter 5

Maria Delmato stood at the stove, stirring a large pot of tomato sauce with a long, wooden spoon. She bent over periodically to smell and taste the sauce, see if it needed anything added to it. Pheeny watched her large backside as she stood in front of the pot.

" I talked to your brother today, he isn't coming to dinner. He is busy in the…oh what did he call it?," She turned her face in profile to Pheeny, frowned. "The U of Mee, something like that. Anyway he cannot come."

"Ma, it's the U.P., the Upper Peninsula of Michigan. Across the lake." She rolled her eyes and shook her head, wondering if her mother was intentionally playing dumb, something Pheeny thought she did to purposely irritate her. She looked out the window past the yard, in the direction of Lake Michigan. She had been up there once to visit Joe.

"Remember Joe worked up there?"

"Yes, yes, I remember. With a bunch of men. Where he expects to meet women I don't know. Always wandering in the woods somewhere," She shook her head, then placed her hand on her hip. "And you, miss career girl. You come across any prospects yet?"

The same old conversation with ma, Pheeny thought. The marriage talk.

"You know my career is important to me. I didn't spend all those years in law school for nothing. Besides, the right guy hasn't come along yet."

Maria was silent for a moment. "I see you have become very clever with that fancy lawyer education of yours, but clever enough to get a man?" She stopped stirring long enough to look at her.

"*Clever enough to get a man?* Please ma, do you hear yourself? In this day and age a woman has more choices available to her besides snaring a man. Enough of this backwards thinking."

"Backwards thinking? What is more important than a family I ask you? Nothing! Of course besides Almighty God," She made the sign of the cross, "And he of course sanctions marriage."

Pheeny started thinking of Kevin Feldstone. They had dated on and off for more than a year. Kevin had been very WASPish. He had been sure of himself and where he was going. He didn't believe in God and had no strong ties to his family. The biggest family tie had seemed to be money. He would vacation with his family in San Tropez during the Christmas holidays, where Pheeny met his parents. They had been very polished and cold. Mrs. Feldstone had commented on her Italian nose. Pheeny had retaliated by commenting on her icy-white hair—snow queen hair she had called it. She and Kevin had broken up shortly after that.

Mama never did like Kevin.

"Then there is your poor father, bless his soul in heaven," She again made the sign of the cross. How would he feel about his children never taking marriage vows?"

Pheeny yawned, suddenly feeling very tired. "Look, I don't want to argue with you."

Maria said nothing.

"You know dad would side with me."

She nodded her head, turned to face her daughter. "Yes, you're right, he would have. He wanted you and Joe to be happy. To succeed in life." She wiped her hands on her apron, then screwed the caps on the basil and oregano.

"You're not getting the fresh herbs from the market? Why not?"

Maria sat next to her. "My leg has been bothering me. I have not gotten out as much as I used to."

"You need to get that checked then."

She waved her hand in dismissal. "It's nothing. Just my arthritis."

"There's things they can give you for that."

"Yes, I'm sure there is. Enough about me, let's talk about you."

Pheeny groaned. "Ma, look, I'm tired. The marriage talk can wait another day."

Maria shook her head. "Not about that." She put her hand over Pheeny's.

"Why are you so tired? Aren't you getting enough rest? Put the job away when you come home."

Pheeny put her face in her hands, rubbed her eyes, then looked at her mother. "It's this case, this guy is a real…bastard, and I'm having a hard time getting anything on him."

She rubbed her hand. "They all are bastards. They never made you so tired before."

"This is different."

"No, you make it different. You take it personally."

Pheeny sighed. "Yeah, you're right. Wrong about the marriage thing, but right about the job." She rubbed her head vigorously, fluffing out her hair.

Her mother laughed and rubbed her hand. She got up from the table and went over to the stove. "The pasta is done."

"Good, I'm starved. After this I'm going right home to bed. I've got an early morning at the office."

Maria shook her head. "No one to go home too, such a pity for you."

"Ma, the marriage talk again."

She held up her hands. "All right, no more marriage talk. Let's eat."

***

Pheeny stared at Sargeants Sanders and Musovich in disbelief. "You mean to tell me that you haven't found anything at all to pin on this guy? Wake up! We're talking murder here."

She had been busting her ass for months now, putting a case together against Durant, assuming the detectives were working as hard as she was. She had enough circumstantial; motive was written all over this guy. Dee Dee Banks had simply been a pawn, and for some reason Durant had to have her murdered.

"What about the coroner's evidence? The forensics? There's got to be something based on the physical evidence."

She knew this had to be the ace in the hole. The crime had been so brutal there was without a doubt bound to be some type of physical evidence. Probably tissue transfer, or some type of fiber that could be traced. Pheeny made a mental note of the agencies she would have to contact to get the evidence processed.

Sanders and Musovich looked at each other. Musovich shuffled his feet and glanced at the clock on the wall above Pheeny's head.

"Ms Delmato, the coroner informed us that there is no conclusive evidence as of yet. He sent some samples to the FBI lab—"

"As of yet! How long does this guy need? He knows the turn around for this kind of evidence! What the hell is he trying to cover up?" Pheeny now wished she had worn more of a demure suit color today, possibly

32

something in brown or gray. This red had the effect of amplifying her persona into a fiery red exclamation point. She often wore the suit to make particularly dramatic points during a trial. Not the effect she wanted right now.

"Ms Delmato, we're doing the best we can. This is a big city, we have a lot of other cases that need evidence collection and follow up. Why should this guy get any special preference? Give it a break already."

Musovich barely glanced at Pheeny as he put his papers in the case folder and got ready to leave. Sanders did likewise. She watched the clock as the seconds ticked themselves off. The wave of anger and frustration was passing. Of course these men didn't feel the same way she did, this was just one more case to them. One more case among many. Many that probably wouldn't be solved.

She sighed "Okay, listen, I understand your point of view. Let's give this thing a rest for a while. My boss has cooled on it quite a bit, and therefore I've been handed all the pieces to deal with. Of course I still think it's important, a high priority case, and not just because of who this guy is," Pheeny bit her lip thinking of a way to end the conversation on a more positive note. "Any murder case is going to take high priority. That's just the way it is."

She took in the detectives, waiting for their response.

"All right Ms Delmato, we'll be talking to ya then." They both nodded, and quickly left. No small talk with these guys, though she didn't really expect any.

She carefully sat down at her desk, trying to gather her thoughts. She ran her hand over the smooth, old wood. Antique oak. It reminded her of her mother's house, sitting in the study with her father. The desk enveloped her, making her feel comfortable. It was something stable, something to rely on. Something firm and good outside of the crazy fickleness of the law.

Everything had seemed right when she had first come here. The law had held purpose for her. There had been a definite right and wrong stamped on the character of how she carried herself, how she delved into these cases. After years of the plea bargains, watching criminals walk, ridiculous juries rendering ridiculous verdicts, she was feeling jaded. Tired of business as usual.

Well this case was going to be different, she thought, I'm trusting my hunches on this one.

The phone rang, making her jump.

"Delmato. Can I help you?"

"Hey sis. Glad to finally get a hold of you. Figured I'd get you before you ran off to lunch. What is it today? Guy down the block kill his wife? Or is it something more upscale and media worthy, some kind of white collar thing?"

"Very funny wise guy. And what is it with you? Have you discovered yet why deer hide during hunting season?," Pheeny impatiently drummed her fingers on the desk. "All right Joe, what gives?"

"What's wrong? Too much stress? Why don't you fly over here and visit me, looks like I'll be here at least a week."

"I can't this time. I'd like too, believe me. Recoup time would be great."

"C'mon, I think it would be good for you. These high stress jobs…well take me for example. There is an extremely important management plan I have to review here, in fact a woman's career is riding on it, yet in lieu of all that I can kick back and smell the roses."

"What are you talking about? Ruining someone's career and smelling the roses, that sounds sadistic to me."

"Oh it's all a matter of perspective. So what's up?"

"This guy, he's guilty as hell. It's so obvious. And of course the whole case revolves around getting some hard evidence. Evidence I feel like I am having to literally pry out of the detective staff around here. They just don't take it seriously."

"Bit the old justice bone?"

"Yeah." A heavy handed knock rattled the glass in her office door. Pheeny grimaced. Who was it this time?

"Gotta go, someone's at the door."

"Keep in mind the offer. A couple of days would do you good."

"Okay. Bye."

"Bye." The empty click sounded in her ear. She held the phone for a second, then gently cradled it in the receiver as the knocking resumed.

Chapter 6

I dreamt of laying frozen in ice, of being unable to move. Finally I felt myself rising to the surface of consciousness. I swam to the top, escaping the numbing cold. My eyes opened to the lace curtains waving gently in a chill breeze. Closing my eyes again I snuggled deeper into my bed, hoping for warmth in the nest of blankets.

Sighing, I rolled over, peering out my doorway to the fireplace in the living room.

The field stone fireplace was the real reason I had decided to rent the cabin. It was composed of many gray, pink and white stones, most the size of footballs. The fireplace's designer had made a flower pattern in the middle of the chimney. Maybe getting tired of the endless layer of rock, something to break up the monotony. You didn't notice the pattern right away, but once discerned by the eye you were always drawn to it.

I jumped up and slammed the window shut. The floor was as cold as ice. Hopping from one foot to the other, I rubbed my arms as my teeth chattered. I needed to get a rug in here. A cascade of plunking noises hit the roof. I frowned, hoping it wasn't those damn squirrels looking for a way in. Movement in front of the window caught my eye. Kyle was standing in front of the house with a fistful of pea pebbles.

"My roof isn't here for your target practice, go get a tin can." I pretended to look stern standing in the doorway with my arms crossed.

"I was just chasing the squirrels away for you. Dad wants to know if you want to come over for breakfast. He said he'd make bacon and eggs." Kyle absently looked in the direction of the house. Darryl was standing in the driveway, engrossed with something underneath the hood of his truck. Kyle stared at me, apparently waiting for an answer.

"Sure, I don't see why not. Let me throw my clothes on and I'll grab a loaf of raisin bread. Give me a few minutes and I'll be right over, okay?"

"Okay!" Kyle grinned and bounded off towards his dad. I watched as Kyle told Darryl I would be coming for breakfast. Darryl looked over and saw me standing in the doorway. He smiled and saluted in my direction. I saluted back.

At least the companionship would take my thoughts off meeting with the fed guy on Monday.

I pushed the thought out of my mind hoping it wouldn't come back. Grabbing my red wool sweater hanging over the rocker, I pulled it over my head. I glanced over at the jar of sugar cubes on the table and thought of giving the horses a treat.

Slamming the door shut behind me, I sauntered down the path which led to the stable. The path was becoming overgrown with fireweed and brambles since Darryl had quit renting the cabin to tourists. Now there was only me, and I didn't traverse the trail enough to keep it in shape.

The door squeaked open and the smell of hay and manure greeted me as I stepped quietly inside. It was a small stable supporting only two horses. Smith and Wesson raised their heads from their grain. Wesson, the smaller black yearling, enjoyed my company more than old Smith, who was set in his ways and only wanted to feed in the morning. Whinnying, Wesson hung his head over the stall, anxious to greet me. Smith grunted in disgust and continued feeding.

I spoke gently to Wesson, rubbing his face, scratching behind his ears. Nuzzling my hand, I gave him the sugar. He went back to munching his hay contentedly while I began brushing him down, running my hand over horse hair and muscle. I rubbed his back until his hair begin to gleam. Wesson enjoyed himself, nodding his head and occasionally turning in my direction.

Carefully placing the brush on a corner beam, I left the stable and quickly walked up to the house. Harvey was sitting at the kitchen table with a rosary in his hand.

"Praise be Clare! We never thought you'd git here!"

One day out of the blue Harvey had just shown up at Darryl's property, wearing a raggedy suit jacket and carrying a patched up bible. We figured he had probably been discharged from a down state mental institution.

Harvey maintained that he had traveled the world, and was now on his way to Alaska. Like a migratory bird he had decided to hang around for a while.

"Yes, praise be Harvey. I'm pretty hungry myself. I'm happy Darryl was so kind to invite me over." Nodding in his direction I noticed that Darryl had slicked his hair back especially for this occasion.

"Clare," Harvey grabbed my hand and ushered me into the chair next to his. "It's the spiritual hunger I'm talking about, not the physical." Harvey's eyes blazed with religious fervor.

"Sorry Harvey. I guess I can't think of things like that without food in my stomach."

Darryl handed me a plate of bacon and eggs. I realized I had forgotten the loaf of raisin bread I had meant to bring over. Kyle busied himself with his eggs and a Hotwheels car. He was making it jump off the end of his fork. Harvey had momentarily forgotten his spiritual hunger and was devouring his eggs wholeheartedly.

"Kyle, put that thing away, remember I said no toys at the table."

"Sorry." Kyle sheepishly dropped the car into his lap.

Darryl kept his eyes on his plate while he chewed.

"You're looking pretty down in the dumps there Darryl. What's up?"

Darryl quickly averted his eyes as if I were reading his thoughts. "A few pranksters have gotten into the traps I have on the creek. It looks to be about three people springing the traps from the sets of foot prints I found. You're the investigative cop around here, could you go take a look?"

"Sure. You'll be first on my agenda after my meeting on Monday morning."

We were all clustered together at the end of the dining room table. The rest of the table sat big and empty, waiting for a big farm family to tromp in from the fields and drop into their chairs, ravenous from working all morning long.

Darryl was eyeing me carefully. "I thought maybe it was those protesters that were hanging down at the Kmart. Remember those yahoos?" He shook his head in disgust. "They hung around for a week, trying to get everyone to sign that bear hunting protest. It could have been them. Hell, they could've been the ones feeding the bears! Little wonder a girl got part ate because of it. So what do you think Clare, was it them or what? I would be interested in hearing your opinion, being a professional and all." Darryl smirked across the table at me.

I studied the rose pattern on my plate, thinking that these must have been Darryl's ex-wife's dishes. "You know I can't comment on that type of information

Darryl." I took my last bite of egg and tried to slough off the anger I felt rising towards him.

"Why? No one needs to know. There's no judge and jury here."

I glared at him, feeling the anger rising into a hard knot in my chest.

Kyle looked over at me and touched my hand. "C'mon Clare, let's go fishing. It's a nice day out."

"Holy fishes for dinner. Loaves and fishes!" Harvey banged his spoon on the table.

"It's just fishing Harvey," Kyle said, rolling his eyes. "Who knows if we'll catch anything."

"Yeah, let's do that." I quickly got up and pushed my chair in. "I'll go grab the fishing rods. Thanks for breakfast Darryl."

He was silent as I walked out of the kitchen, screen door banging behind me.

***

We made our way along a trail through the woods that winded and twisted its way along the river bank. The path was worn to a smooth dirt finish.

"We're almost there."

"I know."

We stopped at a small clearing along the bank where white pines towered above us. The river widened at this spot, and many small logs were caught among the rocks in the water, providing a perfect fishing spot.

"I'm sure we'll catch a big steelhead today." I mentioned with authority, glancing over at Kyle.

"Yeah I guess," He didn't look convinced.

We stood in silence. Kyle stood on one foot and then the other.

40

"Is there something else you want to talk about? Seems like there's something bothering you."

"Naw."

"Naw? Your scaring the fish away jerking around like that."

He smiled.

"I just wish that you'd like my dad more so I could have a mom. I know he likes you." He stared out at the water. The silence stood between us, shadowing us like the towering pines.

"Well," I said, stalling for time until I could think of the right thing to say. "I think that—Suddenly a fish grabbed the hook, pulling the line taut. I quickly jerked up on the rod, securing the fish on the hook. The tension on the rod relayed that this was a fairly big fish. I grabbed Kyle's rod and handed him mine.

"Here you bring this fish in, get some good practice."

"No. I can't. You get it. It's your fish."

"It's a big fish, c'mon, you can do it."

"No." Kyle looked uncertain, afraid to take the rod.

"Kyle! We're going to lose this thing!"

He looked at me and the fish thrashing in the water, then grabbed the rod. He pulled it as hard as he could, rod against his stomach, inching the fish in little by little. "I'm getting it! It's coming!"

"Yeah! Okay, just hold him there."

"Like this?" Kyle had him in close. The fish jumped out of the water.

"Let it out a little, he's going to get off jumping like that." He let out a little line and I grabbed the net.

It occurred to me that it would be nice if I had someone throwing out helpful hints to me. Someone to help guide me in the process of helping this little boy who wanted a mother. Someone to give me a script that would fix everything, a script that encompassed the messy feelings, the painfully untidy feelings that didn't fit into a nice neat little box.

I hauled the fish in and Kyle cracked a smile that split his face wide open.

"Congratulations. I think we have dinner."

I thought that maybe it didn't matter. Maybe all that mattered was that I picked up my line and got on with it.

***

I blinked in the dark and immediately glanced at the clock. Illuminated orange numbers said it was 5:00 am. A full hour before I had to get up. Not that I was surprised, I had been waking up every hour looking at the clock. I jumped out of bed. No use in prolonging the inevitable. I shoved my feet in my slippers and threw my robe on. Glancing out the window I noticed that we had gotten a blanket of snow, probably about five inches or so. Now I would have to leave even earlier to get to the county building.

I stacked the kindling on top of the newspapers and flicked the lighter, touching the newspaper edges with flame. The fire caught and whipped itself into a blaze. I stared into it, hypnotized. Then quickly got up. No need to get caught up in relaxing now, I only needed the warming effects of the fire.

Dressing in my uniform I pulled the belt tight around my waist, slipping it into one more notch than I was used too. I frowned at my reflection in the bedroom mirror thinking how ironic it was that most women would welcome the loss of another belt hole. Time to quit skipping meals. I turned in the mirror surveying my reflection. I felt like an army waif. Sighing, I started to unbutton my shirt and grabbed my lone suit out of the closet.

I walked outside to the truck. Looking towards the big house I noticed tracks in the snow. Darryl had been out to feed the horses. He got up early every day to feed them, sometimes as early as four he told me. The years of working on the farm had instilled in him an early routine. Still, I wondered why he didn't slow down when he could. Kyle definitely needed more time with him.

I got in the truck and turned the ignition. The engine groggily sputtered, then rolled over. The icy cold of the vinyl seat seeped quickly into my bones. I got out and rooted behind the seat for the fake sheepskin covering Darla had given me. The stable door creaked open, and the sound echoed through the stillness of the snow. Footsteps crunched in the snow behind me.

"Hey Darryl, I—" I was cut short by arms encircling my waist. I stood stiff with shock.

"Clare." He mumbled as he buried his face in my hair, nuzzling my neck.

Anger flashed behind my eyes and flooded the rest of my body. I wrenched from his embrace and kneed him in the groin. He fell to the ground on his hands and knees, mouth gaping open.

"Jesus Clare, my goddamn balls!"

"You bastard! How dare you! Just what the hell do you think you're doing?" Shaking, I stepped back towards the truck.

He pushed himself up and staggered to his feet. A slow, shit eating grin crossed his face. "Man woman, you are one tough broad. I sure as hell wasn't expecting *that*," He studied my face a moment, running a hand over his mouth. "But maybe I had it coming. What the hell was I thinking anyway? That you might be as lonely as me? You never bring any guys home," Running a hand through his hair, he chuckled. " Hell, we don't even have to be in love to give ourselves a little medicine, just be in the mood that's all." He extended his hand to me. "Friends?"

I stood there glaring at him, feeling violated. "You are one stupid shit Darryl." Still shaking I turned and got in my truck. I rolled the window down. "You do anything remotely like that again and you'll have more to contend with than just my knee." I rolled the window up and threw the gear in reverse, the truck flew backwards as I stomped on the gas pedal. Darryl stood there, dumbfounded, and I was tempted to give him the finger. I suppose he thought I should be the ever polite Clare.

Numbness crept over me as I turned out of the drive.

"Am I going crazy?" I looked in the rearview mirror, searching my eyes. They stared back at me. Scared.

I pressed my foot on the gas and watched the speedometer creep upward. My throat constricted and I took a gulping gasp of air as the trees whizzed by at break-neck speed. Slowing down close to the county building, I spotted a two track that dipped back in the woods and quickly slipped into it. Covering my face with my hands I felt the tears slip between my fingers. I banged my fist against the steering wheel and lay my head against it a moment. Wiping my nose with the back of my hand I started the truck, then carefully backed it out of the two track.

Chapter 7

Pheeny fell back on the sofa and grabbed the remote off the coffee table. Kicking her shoes off, she rubbed her big toe where a blister was forming. Nothing worse than buying brand new shoes only to have them pinch your feet. Expensive shoes too, Italian calfskin purchased at Saks. Hopefully they would be broken in soon.

She turned the TV on, flipping through the shows, finally settling on a rerun of *LA Law*. As if lawyers were all that polished and glamorous. Or all that thin for that matter, Pheeny thought. She got up from the couch and grabbed a bag of chips off the top of the fridge. Tearing them open she nestled onto the couch and blandly stared at the television. The phone rang and she picked it up. Answering it from some faraway place in her mind. "Hello."

"Ms. Delmato? Josephine Delmato?"

"Yes."

"This is Detective Rancor. I've been working on the Durant case."

"Yes." Pheeny sat up.

"I think we have some information you and your people can use, and it's just as you suspected, Durant had her killed by a hired gun to cover his tracks. We have the killer in custody, a guy named Little John, well, that's what the guy goes by, but his real name is John…"

"Wait a minute! You need to slow down, this information may throw the whole case on its head. Start at square one." She turned the television off.

Detective Rancor cleared his throat. "I'm sorry ma'am, I don't mean to mash all the details together, I just don't want to miss anything."

Pheeny could tell he was green. Usually she had to pry it out an old horse detective. He was right though, she had suspected Durant of hiring someone to do his dirty deed. The only reason she could list him as a possible suspect was that he and Dee Dee could be linked as a couple.

"Well, let's get all the pieces and we'll stick them together somehow. We can't make any assumptions about any of this, although I know it's tempting. So this guy, Little John, how did you get this information from him?"

"We picked him up on a burglary, then he talked in jail. One of our informants gave us the information."

"Okay. What did this informant say?"

"He said that Little John started bragging about the murder, admitted to it. You know how these guys brag about offing people to one another. Just another scalp to this guy, he's an Indian you know."

So, Pheeny thought, so what if he's an Indian? What did that have to do with anything?" She hated it when cops already had the suspect tried and hung. Wasn't that her job?

"Forget what I said about assumptions."

Rancor cleared his throat again. "Now the ball's in your court Ms. Delmato. He's not telling us much. Maybe you can get him to talk more, offer him a plea bargain or something? This burglary he's in for, we got him for maybe five years tops. Court date has been set a few weeks from now."

Pheeny didn't answer. She listened to her thoughts, letting them rush through her. Everything was a jumbled mess. Too many unanswered questions. Time to get to the office so she could think straight. Sitting behind the big oak desk would steady her, bring her home to some answers.

"Ms Delmato?"

"Oh, sorry, lost in thought. Listen, I'm going to get going, if the ball's in my court, it's time for some serious scrimmaging."

Rancor chuckled. "Good luck, the opposing team has a good defense."

"Yeah, I know. I'll be talking to you."

Pheeny hung up the phone and looked over at the clock. The long night was only getting longer.

Chapter 8

Wilfred Durant had an iron will. He wasn't about to let this little bitch get to him. And that's what it was all about anyway, letting her get to him. This police investigation was dying down, just as he knew it would. They had no evidence to pin on him. Now there had been a turn in the investigation, the police had been contacting him again. Do you have this piece of information Mr. Durant? Where were you on this day Mr. Durant? We need to obtain bank records for this period of time Mr. Durant. Bank records!

It was all political posturing. He was sure of that. This Delmato bitch was just some crazy little cunt trying to make a name for herself. What a notch in her belt that would be if she convicted him, another lame legal cronie rising to the top.

What a woman like that needed was a good fuck to keep her in line. A good hard fuck.

Durant rose from his seat when he felt the erection pushing against his pants. He went over to look in the mirror and tidy up a bit, running his hands through his reddish brown hair. Steel gray eyes stared back at him. Not too bad for fifty five, not too bad at all. Very few wrinkles or gray. A good vitamin and work out regime had taken care of that.

He tucked his shirt further in his pants. Nice gray pinstripe, an Armani, went perfect with the khaki trousers. Gave the image of outdoorsiness. Hiking through the woods, that sort of thing. Greenwash was an important part of the real-estate business. It was important to show people you were environmentally friendly. Environmentally friendly developers were given the keys to the kingdom. People were much more willing to let you tear up their land if you pretended to do it in a responsible manner.

His thoughts turned again to Delmato. And then there were those who liked to stand in your way. He would take care of it. A few snags were bound to happen periodically. A few phone calls were in order. Someone in the law enforcement business. The problem was as good as solved.

Chapter 9

I hurried up the steps of the county building, tugging on my jacket to pull it into place. The green wool felt foreign to my fingers. The suit had scratched my skin all the way here. Slowing my walk as I entered the building, I pulled myself up and tried to act contained. My mouth felt dry and metallic.

The room number I was looking for loomed in front of my face in bold black letters. Three zero three. I turned the handle and stepped inside.

A man sat at the long desk writing something. He looked up at me expectantly, pen in hand.

"Are you Mr. Delmato?"

"Yes, I'm Joe Delmato."

"I'm Clare McElroy."

He smiled at me and rose from the table, extending his hand. I shook it, noticing how the blue in his shirt matched his eyes. My face flushed.

I sat down.

"Well first of all Clare, please call me Joe, Mr. Delmato sounds like an old married man." He smiled and shuffled his papers neatly into a pile. "Also, I want you to recognize that I'm not any type of punishing authority. We simply need to review the area management plan and make corrections if need be. This is a team effort, it's not the feds versus the state."

He made it sound so easy. Realizing then that I had been holding my breath, I exhaled. I came here expecting a fight, and now I wasn't sure.

"That all sounds very simple Joe. But what if we disagree? What if we can't come to any management conclusions? I mean, the bottom line is that there is a bear out there eating people, and no one sleeps easily at night with that thought lumbering around in their heads."

He started laughing, a deep hearty rumble. "Clare, we will be here until we come to a general consensus. We're both biologists, we know the issues. And if it takes a while, it takes a while. So be it."

He gazed at me with those blue eyes and I became acutely aware of my body. Shifting in my seat I crossed my legs.

He indicated the pile of papers by nodding slightly. "Now to get started, let's look at the total habitat area for black bear. Is there enough? And if there is not enough, what can we do about it?"

I pointed to an area on the management map, the area allocated to black bear. "Well look, bear have ample habitat. That's not a problem. So far. But I think one of the main concerns is human encroachment, bear having these huge ranges. People live on the edge of their habitat, and people have been known to feed bears. And it seems to be getting out of control." I paused a moment, running my hand through my hair. "That's essentially the problem, animal and human conflicts. Disneyfying the animals so to speak."

He regarded me a moment, smiling. "Disneyfying. I like that word, you make it up?"

"Yeah. Look, I came in here with a rehearsed speech, and I intended to deliver it just as I had it memorized in my head. But I can't do that. I think what I need to do is lay it on the line and tell you how I feel about the problem. That's all. Why hide behind the bureaucratic protocol?"

He was watching me with a quizzical expression, probably thinking I'd flipped my lid. I was starting to wonder about my sanity again.

"Well Clare," he said, putting the stack of papers in his briefcase. "I too would like to cut through agency red tape and lay it all on the line. I do have to go through a certain amount of protocol, as I know you do, but it's nice to know we recognize the problem in congenial terms."

"What are we going to do then? Aside from filling out the forms, dotting the i's and crossing the t's? The real issue is that I have a human eating black bear on my hands, and the humans are scared."

"Then I suppose people management is at hand, rather than managing for the wildlife?"

"Maybe." In my years of being a scientist I had been taught to be neutral. I had the skills to manage animals, but people? I didn't think so. "Of course," I continued, "We also need to dispose of the bear. Kill it." I corrected myself.

"One male amongst many, though it probably was a juvenile." He said.

"Yes, my thoughts exactly. I do have a lead, however tenuous. There is a trapper who says he knows this bear, this old guy who lives outside of town. We can start by talking to him."

"All right, I'll take your lead. We can find him after lunch."

Glancing up at the clock on the wall I was amazed to see that the hands stood straight up at noon, time had gotten away from me. Maybe I was enjoying myself.

The road to Fisher Black's cabin was bumpy and long. It started from an old logging two track, continued through the woods for about ten miles, then dwindled to nothing. Trees encroached on either side, taking over the trail by converging in the middle.

"I think we're going to have to hoof it from here on in." I placed the truck in park and got out.

We had decided to start the next morning after our meeting. I figured Fisher might be gone during the day. Like most wild things he was probably holed up sleeping somewhere during daylight hours.

"Where did you hear of this guy?" Joe pulled his jacket collar up around his ears. A cold northern wind was beginning to blow off Lake Superior. Even in the shelter of the forest the brisk chill was biting into us.

"I met him a while ago, a friend told me about him."

There were some illegal traps set along the river that I had been pulling out for a week or more. I had found them during the day, only to have them put back the following morning. At the end of my rope, I was about to confiscate them entirely and quit the in the river, out of the river game. Darla had mentioned he lived at the end of the old logging trail and liked to be left alone. What hermit didn't?

Setting out the next day determined to find him, I had walked for miles. When I first started out I had felt irritated that I was actually going to a person's home to have him buy a trapping license. Towards the end of the walk I was feeling more peaceful. There was a new found respect growing in me that this man had chosen to live his life so far from civilization. He literally was miles from the nearest road, those lifelines of our civilized blood. I thought of all the times tourists neglected to travel down bumpy dirt roads to find, maybe, what they might be looking for. They always stayed on the blacktop.

When I had gotten to Fisher's cabin I had humbly paid the money for his license and fastened it to his door. I didn't bother to leave a note.

Joe and I walked in our own rut down the old road. Neither of us spoke for a while. I was glad he didn't feel the need to fill in every nook and cranny of silence with some inane comment.

The wind didn't blow as hard in the forest interior, conifers were packed tightly together, acting as an insulating factor. Aspen and birch gave way to tamarack and fir. The tamarack had turned a flaming yellow, giving the forest color when the deciduous trees lost their leaves. I noted the animal activity, porcupine droppings next to tree holes and the sawdust where they had been gnawing. Buck rubs along trees. No sign of bear. Yet.

I started looking for the path that led off the two track and into Fisher's camp.

There was a story of a couple of adventurers who had managed to find Fisher's camp. They had thought it quaint to find a hunting lodge so far back in the woods. Setting their tent nearby, they had settled down for a few days camping. Hearing strange noises in the middle of the night that sounded more animal than human, they had huddled together in their tent afraid for their lives. They had it figured for a psycho's camp, and they were next in line to be dismembered and eaten.

At daybreak they made a beeline for town. After a few beers to sooth their jangled nerves, they spilled their terrified tale. Moe listened carefully to what they had to say and agreed that there were some strange people in the northern woods, but most were harmless. He had not wanted to betray the old hermit's identity.

"I've heard he's psychic, this hermit guy." I glanced over at Joe.

"Oh?" He didn't seem interested.

He then tripped over a tree root but managed to catch himself before he fell face down on the trail. I burst out laughing, and he quickly joined in.

I held my hand to my mouth. "Sorry."

"No offense taken. You can tell I haven't been out in the woods in a while, I've got wooden feet. I used to work up here you know, northwest of here a little, in the Porkies," He looked at me a little forlornly. "I envy you."

"Envy?" I suppose I could see why. Who wouldn't want to be in the field instead of behind a desk all day?

"Yeah. In fact I had this scenario worked out in my mind about you. I figured you to be some halfwit the state had put up here. You know how affirmative action is." He smiled at me sheepishly.

"No, I don't know how affirmative action is."

I spied the clearing up ahead. We entered cautiously, looking for signs of life. The hermit didn't appear to be anywhere in the camp. There were a couple skins stretched out in various states of being cured, one was a deer and the other a mink. I noted he did use civilized tools, something I hadn't seen on my last visit. There was an ax stuck in a chopping block and a large hunting knife protruded from the side of the cabin.

We looked around uneasily. I had no clue as to when he left or when he would be back. It felt timeless in this little clearing, like the invention of the clock was a long way off. I half expected to see notches in a cabin log marking the days gone by.

"I guess I'll leave a note," I began half-heartedly. "I don't know if we can expect him to meet with us on a particular day, or even if he wants to."

"No, not really. I'd rather not meet with you now that you mention it."

I spun around to see Fisher standing there in the clearing. My gut felt like someone had physically pushed me.

"How long have you been spying on us?" Irritated, I put my hands on my hips.

He stared at me a few seconds, making me feel as if he could see right through me.

He busied himself with his skins and then set about making a fire as if we didn't exist for him. Joe and I looked at each other. He shrugged, as if to say; 'this is your show.'

"You know what we're here for?" I asked.

He nodded.

A blanket of silence fell over the campsite. In this timeless spot I was beginning to get uncomfortable.

"C'mon Fisher, why don't you just tell us what we need to know? What about the bear? We've come this far."

"What you want will be awake in spring. It will be a time of new growth for you. And for you too." He nodded in Joe's direction.

I snorted with contempt. "Yeah, so? The bear is hibernating. Big news. I didn't need to come all the way out here for you tell me that."

"I'm not a fortune teller!," he snapped. "Before the new growth they'll be a bit of death in your life. But that's the way it is. Death then birth." He scratched his chin and looked over at me. I looked away. He was making me uncomfortable. Probably just trying to scare me.

Then without so much as a glance in our direction he lay down in front of the campsite fire and lowered his hat over his face. Within minutes he was snoring.

Chapter 10

Moe had never seen anything like it. The guy had walked in here claiming he was Clare's brother. And an alcoholic on top of that. He had sat himself down at the bar, ordered coke after coke, and delighted the locals with stories about his drinking days. He had even bought everyone a few rounds of beers.

Moe was beginning to wonder if he was in a manic phase. Alcoholics were pretty unbalanced to begin with and tended to get a burst of energy when they had just quit drinking. Still, he didn't seem like the dangerous type.

"Hey Moe, another round for my new friends."

Moe could of sweared that there was some sort of mental telepathy going on between the drunks in his bar and the ones outside, because now they were starting to pour in in twos and threes. The bar wasn't usually this full until at least four o'clock, happy hour.

"Don't you think you should slow it down a little kid? I don't need my town liquored up before noon."

The kid laughed. He had hazel eyes and a medium build. Hair the same color of Clare's, chestnut. He looked like the boy next door, all cleaned up, but with an old holey jean jacket, and a pack of Marlboros in the top pocket. He proceeded to tap one out and light it up. Boy was Clare going to be surprised.

"Hey kid, what's your name again?"

"Dan."

"Okay Dan, could you come over here for a minute?" Moe motioned for him at the end off the bar where he had been polishing glasses.

"Dan, I hate to put a little damper on your being the life of the party and all, but in the context of alcoholic behavior, well like I said I've been sober for going on ten years now and studying to be a therapist…" He trailed off when he knew he had started to ramble, still hadn't gotten that therapeutic succinctness down yet. Probably from years of drinking and evading issues, skirting around them so to speak.

Dan was watching him intently, eagerly, almost hanging on every word. The kid did seemed to be eating it up. His eyes were fiery and glazed, he was such an animated person. Moe wondered if he knew about the hard work he had ahead.

"What we talk about in Alcoholics Anonymous kid, I mean Dan, is balance. And right now you're not showing me a whole lot of balance. If I were you I'd get off my high horse and get myself together. You just got here from far away, down state, the big city. You need to relax, put your thoughts in order. You have got a lot to tell your sister. Of course, not to be preaching or nothing."

He avoided sermonizing at any cost. Moe hated preachers. His first sponsor in AA had been a preacher. The man had Moe going to some Bible revival meeting every time he turned around. After so many do this, don't do that, he had given up. One day he found himself with a beer in his hand, just to relax, he told himself. That had kicked off another six months of hard drinking. He had learned his lesson. No more preaching.

"Yeah. You're so incredibly right Moe. I need to get more balance and prepare myself for Clare. I know she will think this is so impulsive, but it's good to live your life you know, take risks. It was time to change the people in my playpen. So here I am! Slapping the table and laughing, he then looked directly at Moe. "And I would like it very much if you were my sponsor."

Moe felt honored and at the same time a little uneasy. He knew the AA sponsorship could turn into a nightmare. He wasn't quite sure of the kids behavior yet. Was he gonna call him in the middle of the night? Was he gonna get all screwy, asking Moe about his every move? He gave the kid a cold, hard appraisal. There was something authentic about him Something honest. Moe felt he could trust him even though he knew he would never trust the disease of alcoholism. There was something in the kid he could take on.

And poor Clare. What was she gonna think? Her brother had just shown up out of the blue, and it sounded like he intended to stay for a while. He hoped it would work out.

"All right kid, I'll take you on."

"Great! I promise I won't disappoint you." Dan reached across the bar, grabbed Moe's face in his hands and smacked a kiss on his mouth. Everyone within viewing distance howled with laughter.

Moe wiped his mouth with the back of hand. "Okay kid, don't go tripping all over yourself. We have to set some ground rules," Moe looked at the kid sternly, and crossed his beefy arms. Above him hung a rack of moose antlers. "First of all, no calling me past ten at night."

"No problem, I go to bed at that time anyway." Dan nodded.

"Second, I don't want to see you hanging out in this place. That'll start you off to a relapse quicker than falling off a bar stool."

"Hey, isn't that kind of hypocritical? I mean you're an alcoholic and you work here. Hell, you own this bar! And it looks to me like the place is the center of life in this town." Dan glanced around.

Moe widened his eyes. The kid sure had some nerve! Still, he admired spunk. It showed spirit, like he had a mind of his own rather than some mindless do gooder, never making waves. A mark of an independent spirit.

"Well you got me there. I guess we can pass on that one. Besides, I can keep an eye on you."

"Sure Moe, keep an eye on me." He gave a wink, jumped of the bar stool and headed out the door.

So he was gonna be that kind, always testing. Moe shook his head and wiped the counter top down. A smile was beginning to creep across his face in spite of everything.

Chapter 11

I drove as carefully as I could, but my mind was bent on daydreaming. I felt spacey, out of order. A few times I had to actually jerk the steering wheel away from side of the road. I kept coming back to the fact that Joe wasn't what I had pictured, that nothing was what I had originally pictured. No, this wasn't a fat, uptight, by the book, federal government worker. He was genuinely a nice guy willing to push the rule book aside and work on the problem from a fresh perspective. He was also very cute. Grinning, I again swerved the truck away from the ditch.

Pulling into the meandering drive leading to my cabin, I noticed Darryl's truck in front of the big house. I slowly pulled around his section of drive hoping he wouldn't hear the tires in the gravel.

Kyle sat on the stump in front of the cabin. The stump where I split wood. Darryl had tried to get me to use his huge cache of wood, and had even offered to drive a cord over in his truck a few days ago, but I had refused. Now I wish I had taken him up on the offer. It would give me an excuse to go over there and talk to him about the incident this morning.

When he walked through my door I wasn't sure whether I had actually thought him into existence and he would vanish when the thought escaped me, or he was a viable human being. I blinked hard. But there he stood.

"Clare, your mouth is hitting your chest. I'm not green or anything am I? I'm sure I look the same as I did five years ago." He nervously took his hands and smoothed the hair away from his face, the same honey colored version of mine, except ponytailed.

"How did you get in here, and more importantly, what in the hell are you doing here?"

"Clare, is that appropriate talk for a child's ears? And like, when have you *ever* locked this place?"

Kyle stood next to Dan. He looked like he had found his long lost buddy.

"Can you just please give me a straight answer?"

"I had to get out of there, just had to leave. That place was driving me totally crazy. I truly thought I would start drinking again, and you know the old man, always riding me. He just never lets up, like I'm one of his military cronies. So one day I woke up, just really woke up, ya know? Like I had an epiphany or something, and I thought hey, Clare's got it together, nice place, beautiful setting. You have to tell me you missed me a little! Oh, and uh, Darryl, invited us over for dinner. You two have a little something going?" He smirked at me.

He just stood there looking at me like all was well with the world, and all he needed was a place to hang his hat for a while.

I chose to ignore his little jab. "Dan, what are you asking me? To stay here? I don't have room."

"Please Clare, just for a few months. I have nowhere else to go."

"I don't know."

"I promise, I'll do anything."

"I just don't know!" I yanked the door open and Dan was hot on my heels. I felt a pounding headache coming on.

"Clare, just relax a minute and listen to what I've said."

"No Dan, you listen. Do you even comprehend anything about a normal life? You can't just show up here expecting me to take care of you. It doesn't work that way. You need to learn how to stand on your own two feet. You're just like mom."

I stood there glaring at him, vaguely hoping he would reel from the venom in my words. But instead of being shocked or angry, he calmly sat at the kitchen table and gazed out the window, surveying the huge white pine in front of the cabin.

"You're right. Totally right. I don't want to be like mom, and here I am an alcoholic. Do you think I want to die like her?"

He looked at me with pleading eyes, taking me totally off guard. He was the last of my family. The only one that I could ever halfway talk to. Could I deny him a chance at having some kind of life?

I had forgotten about Kyle. He was sitting over at the table, looking at Dan and I expectantly.

"Well what do you think Kyle, you ever see grown people argue?"

"Yeah." Looking down at the table he started making figure eights with his finger. He kept running his finger through the small dip I had inadvertently created when the table was being refinished.

"I wish Harvey wasn't up at the house. He smells." Kyle wrinkled up his nose.

"Who's Harvey?"

"He's the local crazy guy. I guess in the old days he would have been called the village idiot. He stays with different people around town. Now he's up at Darryl's."

"Yeah, and he's making my dad mad. He keeps bumping into stuff in the kitchen. Dad told him to get out and he sat down and stared."

I knew what he was talking about. It was the kind of stare he would get into when he went inside himself to a place that no one knew. Some place safe.

"You're going to love it here," I said sarcastically. "And this will be your initiation." I pulled my chair back in a frustrated huff. Dan met my eyes for a brief second. He registered a silent thank you.

"You can stay here, but let's get this straight - you are getting a job and you can stay only as long as it takes to save up and move out of here. Got it?" I held his eyes with a level gaze.

"I'll do everything you want. I promise."

***

I sat staring out the window, slumped in a chair at Darla's kitchen table. "I think I'm losing my mind."

Darla looked up from peeling an apple. Her paring knife evenly circled the fruit as she watched my face.

"You're not losing your mind, just going through a transition. That's all."

"That's *all?* Yeah well, if your crazy alcoholic brother came back to haunt you, your landlord hit on you, your career was in crisis—I'm sure you would feel the same way." I crossed my arms and looked out the window again. Darla's nieces and nephews played some sort of chase game in the yard. The older kids were directing everything. Their yard was threadbare, but a few clumps of grass hung on here and there, desperately clinging to survival.

Some people in town said that the reservation was a shambles, that it was disgusting the way trash piled up around the houses. I thought it looked comfortable. No one seemed to care if the cars invaded the lawn, or that the wash hung from a car. It was a friendly, easy

64

hodgepodge of things and people. My military father would have had a silent fit at the sight of it all.

"Sometimes transitions are hard to take, especially the one you're experiencing. You're getting hit all at once."

"You can say that again, within the span of a few days. One more day of this bear interview, then it will be over. This guy though, he's not what I expected. He's actually pretty understanding, and get this, we even went out to find Fisher, see if he had any news about the bear."

"What's he saying about the bear? He's not saying you have to trap it is he?" Darla dumped another load of apples into the ten gallon pot. She was making pork and apple stew.

"Nah, are you kidding? Well, the thought did cross my mind a while back and then I realized how ridiculous that would be. Picture it; trapping every bear within a fifty mile radius and putting radio collars on all of them. No way. He wants to get as much information as possible on this particular animal, and educate the public regarding bear safety."

"Education?" Darla's ears perked up. "What about some type of public meeting? We could put fliers around town, and you could show slides. We could use this meeting as a stepping stone for other conservation issues." She grabbed another apple and enthusiastically started paring it.

"I'll need to discuss it with Joe. The idea of a meeting is good, but I don't want to throw every conservation topic under the sun in there. I know how that would turn out."

"All right then, it's a start anyway." Darla looked hurt. "Bring it up and see what he thinks. Maybe he could partake in the educational festivities. What's he like anyway? You sound very personable already. First name basis and all." She gave me a sly smile and lit a cigarette.

The smoke drifted in ringlets above her head than moved towards the window. I watched as it momentarily tried to find a way to escape, then dissipated.

I thought I might counter Darla's suggestion with a laugh, cover my feelings by brushing it off. I didn't really know how I felt. I felt a rush, the intense feeling you get when you know you like a member of the opposite sex. And sex, well, it had been a long time.

"Okay. I'll admit it, I like him. A little. God, Darla, he beats half the guys here in White Cloud, missing teeth and spitting tobacco at the nearest hole in the ground."

She laughed. "Too bad he lives in Chicago."

"Too bad." I didn't want to think about it. Besides, a relationship was out of the question.

Since moving here I had become entrenched in my job, wearing my damn uniform so often it was starting to feel like a second skin. A skin that in some ways was becoming too much of my personality. A personality I didn't know if I enjoyed, or even felt comfortable with for that matter. There was no reason for me to think of much else besides the job. Maybe now I had a reason.

"What are you smiling at? Are you mentally undressing this guy?" She blew smoke over my head.

"Oh nothing really," I blinked and rubbed my eyes, staring at her vacantly for a moment. "How on earth did I ever get into this line of work? I mean really, a city girl from Detroit. What was I thinking?"

"I don't know. Why did you get into this line of work? For the great selection of men up here?" She started laughing.

"I didn't get into it for the bears that eat humans aspect, that's for sure. It seems so ridiculous, this whole bear tragedy. The whole incident just smacks of human stupidity. What do people think is going to happen if they feed wild animals? They're not tame for God's sake. I just don't get it, don't get it at all. People need to learn their place in the natural world, which of course doesn't entail feeding wild animals like zoo pets. Once bears become habituated to people feeding them, it's just a matter of time before the bear decides to taste the hand that feeds it."

Darla was silent a moment, watching me. A smile crept over her face. "I always knew you had it in you."

"In me?"

"Yes, in you. Something that's hard to learn, but some people just have in them, you know, the native view of things. Seeing the natural world for what it is, and knowing your place in it. As a human being that is."

"I don't get it."

Darla adjusted her glasses, threw a pared apple into the pot and grabbed another one. "You will."

Chapter 12

Pheeny raced up the steps, her navy pumps clicking out a staccato beat. Today she was the epitome of judicial discretion, somber navy blue suit with a crisp white shirt underneath. No need for red today, no need to upset the prisoners. She hated the feeling of being ogled by the male prisoners, they all acted like they hadn't seen a woman for a million years, and in this degraded state of affairs basic social decency didn't apply. And it was hard to hide her voluptuous form. Even in this suit.

She remembered a particularly trying trial where she had run the gamut of suits and dresses of every conceivable color. Every day was a presentation, and every outfit had to match impeccably with the point she would be making for the day. She had paraded in white linen, silk chemise, and black chiffon. She had theatricized in lace, and bantered and cajoled in plaid. She had been flushed, wide eyed and loving it. For the entire case Pheeny knew she was a born trial lawyer.

After words, a photographer had caught up with her amongst the throngs of people on the court house steps. He was beautifully chiseled, with a cleft chin and muscled arms. A living Adonis. She was instantly attracted to him when he had approached her, feeling the blood rush to her face. But then trials always had the tendency to make her horny. She figured it was the adrenaline.

Then he mentioned what *kind* of photographer he was, gave her a seductive smile and licked his lips. She whacked him over the head with her briefcase and it had sprung open, papers flying everywhere. Just by chance a reporter had snapped the shot at the moment of impact. It had made front page news.

She grimaced at the thought, thinking of her family's reactions. Joe had found it amusing, saying the guy was just another male slut. He had given her his; 'I'm just a boy at heart' grin. Expecting sympathy from her mother, she was disappointed. Maria had simply bemoaned the fact that there were no good men available nowadays, little wonder Pheeny was still single.

Why did men seem to think they could play by different sexual rules anyway? Modern day society sure hadn't seemed to have evolved much. She would never had said anything so disgusting. Maybe she should have. But what would that prove? That she could look at a man like a piece of meat and treat him disrespectfully. She shook her head in disgust. Sometimes she felt as if men did not see women for who they were, just people like them. They were always taking women's sexuality and twisting or controlling it.

She stood in front of the reception desk, waiting in line. It was always interesting to watch the number of people waiting in line to see the prisoners. And it was always surprising to see the sheer number of women. Obviously these guys had people who loved them, that or these woman could not pry themselves out of a bad relationship. The latter was a more likely scenario

Women with children in tow. Pheeny felt sorry for them. All their hopes and dreams pinned on some loser. What a shame.

A woman in front of Pheeny held a little girl who was intently staring at her and sucking her thumb. She had short curly hair and was wearing a floral print dress with white socks and black patent leather shoes. Pheeny smiled and gave a little wave. The little girl buried her face in her mother's neck She wondered what it would feel like to have a little girl bury her face in her neck, then quickly dislodged the thought. Not in this lifetime.

She impatiently glanced at her watch. The appointment wouldn't take long. She needed to determine if there was a possible case against this guy, or if the detective was babbling on for nothing. Pheeny carefully scanned the file in front of her. She might as well, as slow as these prison personnel were in sifting through the visitors.

She took a deep breath and curled and uncurled her toes in her pumps like a cat flexing its claws. They felt too tight.

John Wesley Whelan, a Chippewa from the Sault Tribe. The guy didn't seem to have too much of a rap sheet, mostly petty burglaries. He had done time on two previous accounts, but nothing more than a year. A few drug convictions. All of this was good for him, the judge would look favorably on someone who had a fairly clean record. The prisons were overcrowded with far worse than this.

But murder was a big jump from petty crime. The question of motive wasn't readily apparent in the file, and if there was no motive or hard evidence associated with this guy, well, that was that. No case. No trial. No nothing. The legal system couldn't be bothered with it.

She thought again of Dee Dee.

Who was going to bat for these women? Time after time she had seen these cases getting shoved into the circular file only to do just that. Circulate. It made it look like something was being done. They were given low priority, and as much she hated to admit it, the system was biased in favor of wealth. Ms Dee Dee Banks happened to be in the lower income range.

So many murders, so many women.

Pheeny wondered fleetingly if any of these women here knew that. The thin woman in front of her holding the little girl in the floral dress was being escorted to a small sitting area with the other women to wait. Presumably they would all be led in at once to the visitation area.

Pheeny was next in line.

"Josephine Delmato, assistant DA. I have an appointment with Mr. John Whelan."

"Oh, Miss Delmato," The receptionist gave her the once over reserved for those in the public eye. "You look much smaller in person. Also much, um, more bodacious."

Pheeny gave her the deadpan look. She had learned a long time ago to let it all pass. People just seemed to think it was their unalienable right to comment on your appearance if they saw you on television.

"Yeah, the network made me get a boob job to increase their ratings. Everything is a conspiracy ya know, we're all in it together, the DA's office, the network, the game shows…shall I go on?"

The receptionist quickly took her eyes off Pheeny's chest and busied herself with the schedule roster. "Yes, here you are. Follow the guard and you will be escorted to a visiting room."

"Thank you very much." Pheeny picked up her briefcase and shoved the Whelan file inside.

"Ms. Delmato?" The receptionist looked pained.

"Yes?" Pheeny turned and waited.

"What I meant to say was; *nice suit.*" She smiled, turning two shades of red.

Pheeny smiled back. "Thanks."

She followed the guard down the gray hallway. They came to a door and he fumbled with a set of keys hooked to his waist.

"An hour Ms. Delmato?"

"Yes."

"This guy is supposedly dangerous but I don't think he'd hurt a fly. Tough guy act is all. You get so you can read 'em quite well in here. I'll have to sit and wait in the corner for your protection."

She noticed he had a gun in his holster.

"Sure, no problem."

She entered with the guard as the key clicked in the lock. Whelan sat in his chair looking up at them. His arms were crossed on the table, with burly tattoos on either bicep. His hair was long and black, twisted into a single braid down his back. Pheeny was taken back by his size. The file read 6'3, two hundred fifty pounds, but it was just a statistic until you saw the numbers fitting securely in the shape of a human being.

"Mr. Whelan, I'm Josephine Delmato, assistant District Attorney. I trust you know the nature of my visit?" Pheeny extended her hand and sat on the rickety chair opposite Whelan. The guard contented himself in the corner with a murder mystery.

"Yeah, I know who you are and why you're here. Why don't we just cut to the chase - I don't know nothing, and I didn't do it."

Pheeny watched his face. A big beefy face with tired brown eyes that registered no malice.

"You didn't do it? I find that, well, hard to believe. The detective I spoke with said he has some pretty heavy circumstantial that you did do it. But you haven't been prosecuted yet, and of course your innocent until proven guilty. I have every faith in the American justice system."

Whelan stared at her. His face did not betray his emotions, regardless of what he was feeling. "The American justice system sucks."

"Excuse me?" Pheeny expected to hear more expounding on his supposed innocence.

"You heard me. Why do you think I'm here? I've been set up. I'm just a little pawn in a big game. A little cog in a wheel that you Anglos set in motion a long time ago."

"I'm not an Anglo Mr. Whelan, I'm Italian."

"Same diff."

"No. No it's not. Anglo Saxons were a Tribe of Germanic peoples while my Tribe…oh forget it." She shook her head, on the verge of getting angry.

"I suggest you take this seriously, you are a suspect. I need as much information as possible of what you know of the Dee Dee Banks murder case."

"Ms. Delmato, like I said, I didn't do it, and that's all I can tell you. This whole thing is going to turn into a big race war, that's why they picked an Indian. It's a cover up."

"Who's they? What are you talking about? This fabrication is going to get you nowhere Mr. Whelan. We've got some our best detectives on this case, and a whole slew of specialists. If you're the murderer, believe me, the evidence will prove it."

Pheeny impatiently tapped her pencil on the desk. "If you have nothing else to tell me Mr. Whelan, I won't waste your time or mine. I'll be going."

Pheeny stood up to leave. She put the file carefully in the briefcase and paused a moment. Her eyes met Whelan's for a brief second, then she looked away. She turned towards the door. The guard snapped his book shut and stood up.

"Ms. Delamato?"

"Yes, Mr. Whelan?" Pheeny stood in the doorway, looking back. Whelan regarded her with amusement. "I admire your work and I wish you the best of luck on this case. If you catch the guy, you'll be doin' all of us a favor."

"Thanks for the meeting Mr. Whelan, it's been a pleasure." She quickly shut the door and clicked down the hallway. Turning the corner towards the lobby she thought of all the useless games prisoners played. Never once realizing who held all the cards.

***

Pheeny opened the door and winced as a volley of camera flashes went off in her face. She knew there would be some newspeople, but nothing of this caliber. Trying to get her bearings, she judged the distance between herself, her car, and the insatiable reporters. Realizing the crowd contained at least fifty people, she faltered.

"Ms. Delmato, is it true that Little John is Dee Dee's killer?"

"What happens next in this case?"

"When will we have any real information?"

"Will this case thrust you into a good political position regarding the DA's office?" A few chuckles from the male camera hounds.

The questions were flying hard and fast, and she knew that unless she gained control of the situation, the press could force her into saying something stupid. That was the key with these people, unless you gained control, they would devour you.

She stopped and adopted her most serious camera face. "I'm sorry that I won't be able to give you any statement today that leads us in the direction of solving this heinous crime. Mr. John Whelan, contends he has an alibi for the period in question. We in the district attorney's office will of course verify that information. Thank you." Pheeny started inching forward towards her car. Not too far now, about ten feet, give or take a few.

"Is it true that you have had sexual relations with Lyle O'Malley, to help further your career?"

She couldn't help herself, the guy was directly in front of her smirking. She dug her heel directly into the toe of his sneaker.

"Ow!"

"That is not true! Lyle and I are colleagues, and that's as far as it gets."

"Can you explain then why the two of you were seen at dinner, and he was rubbing your arm?"

Now they had her. Once you reacted emotionally to a question they waited like a pack of hungry dogs poised for the kill. Pheeny felt like kicking herself, or stepping on her own foot for that matter.

"Ms. Delamato, one more thing, how do you feel this case will help women's rights?"

Pheeny felt her heart start to thud and her face flush. Here was a guy who actually cared about women's issues. She turned and there he was, a guy with a backwards baseball cap, bent over a notebook. He looked up expectantly, eyes meeting hers.

"Well, Mr...."

"My name is Cole Potter, I'm with *The Independent News*."

"Mr. Potter, that is the first intelligent question I've heard today, and if you would like, I'll give you an exclusive interview."

His jaw dropped. "Sure Ms. Delmato, it would be an honor."

Pheeny beamed at him, linked her arm through his and escorted him past the throngs of news people to her car. Behind her she could hear the click of a hundred cameras.

***

The coffee bar must have been built before the Chicago fire or right afterwards. The ceilings were high and ornate scroll work lined the ceiling edges. A few writers were scattered amongst the tables. It gave the place a touch of angst. Angst and something more, Pheeny couldn't quite put her finger on it. Maybe it was intellectualism, that studious quality that attracted intelligent types to places like these. Pheeny liked to think that people in the legal profession could inspire that type of atmosphere, but that wasn't always so. For the most part they were simply deal makers.

Cole was giving her a run down on how he wound up in Chicago. He was originally from a poor, working class section of Cincinnati, and his mother had convinced him to go to college. He said he had always wanted to write. Working his way through school, he worked on the campus newspaper, then had wrote for a newspaper in Cinci, and had finally landed a job at *The Independent*, the perfect paper for him. He said he was fed up with the discrepancies he saw between rich and poor, and the lies the media told to uphold those divisions. Dedicated to fight for the underdog, he wanted nothing more than to report the truth.

"Am I boring you?" Cole looked at her quizzically as he chewed on the end of his straw. He had ordered black coffee with creamer, complaining the foo foo coffee was for the up and coming crowd. He had one of those honest open faces that couldn't hide anything. A face that was smattered with freckles.

"No, no, of course not. It's just that this case is wearing me out. I never expected it to last this long."

Cole nodded. "Yeah, since I've been at *The Independent,* I've sort of kept tabs on this story. Quite a few twists and turns with a few of the suspects."

Pheeny nodded. "Exactly. I just don't have the time to devote to it that I would like. You know," Pheeny lowered her voice and surveyed the room, "I have got this theory, and of course it's only a hunch, women's intuition, call it what you want, but I know who did it, but I just can't pin it on him. The guy is elusive and slips through my fingers like sand."

"Are you telling me this off the record then?" He raised his eyebrows.

"Hell no! Like I would trust the press. Of course you can print this if you want. The more media I get the better. Gotta keep this case alive."

She took a sip of her coffee and looked around. Men in suits clustered at the center table. Pheeny recognized them from City Hall, making or breaking deals, she assumed.

She took another sip of coffee and looked at Cole. "You wanted to know how I felt this case related to women's issues, and wasn't just some tabloid center piece the rest of the press would like to portray it as? Well, I'll tell you Cole, nobody gives a shit about little two bit Dee Dee Banks. Maybe because I'm a woman I consider it my duty to protect the downtrodden, which usually happens to be women."

She stopped long enough to glare at him and take the last sip of coffee. He met her eyes and didn't look away. She took that as a good sign. He wasn't put off at the force of her anger.

"I'm going to get him, and that's that." She pushed her cup towards the middle of the table. Unlike Cole she had ordered foo foo coffee. She loved it, especially hazel nut.

"I kind of figured it was your nature to fend for the poor and unwanted." He surveyed his hands spread out on the table. "I wish I could say my motives were so pure. My sister was raped, I understand what that means, how a life can be so screwed after that. I guess you can say I woke up and smelled the coffee. Thank God she wasn't murdered." He shook his head.

Pheeny studied him. He certainly seemed sincere. She started feeling irritated with herself, this job was making her much too jaded. She realized she didn't tell Cole who she thought committed the murder.

"Yeah, I believe it's Durant too."

"How did you know what I was thinking?"

He laughed. "You get good at reading people after a while. Besides I've dug up a few things, and I also have my own personal theory." He winked at her.

"Well spill it Mr. Potter. Let's compare notes."

"I do know that Durant and Dee Dee were seeing each other, a fact that he has tried to conceal since this investigation began."

"I got that one."

"And she found out about one of his secrets."

"I suspected that." Pheeny nervously twisted her straw around her finger. Maybe he was actually on to something. "Spit it out! What secret?"

"I don't know, that's as far as I've gotten."

Pheeny slumped back in the booth. At least this guy was a go getter, you'd have to give him that.

"Well Cole, it's good to see we're both on the same wavelength. Why don't we pool our info and fashion it into some kind of article. I'm sure I have got a few details you haven't heard of yet. As they say, two heads are better than one." She smiled half- heartedly. Better luck next time.

"I think that's a good idea Josephine, but I think I can do you one better."

"What's that?"

"Why don't we start collaborating? Work together on this thing. I do some free lancing, and I'm sure I can get some other papers to pick up on the story, it all depends on the slant I give it."

"All right Cole, that would be fine. Understand though, that I've got priorities other than this one case."

She cocked her head and examined him. He was grinning at her like the guy from *Mad* magazine.

"I'm glad you find it amusing that we have a shit load of work to do."

His grin faded and he regarded her seriously. "It's not the work load that I find amusing. The thing is I know we'll solve this case. Believe me, it will happen. I can feel it."

Chapter 13

I had traveled all the way to Green Bay and bought a peach colored suit. The fabric felt soft against my skin, sensuous, managed to hug all the right spots, and it accented my coloring nicely. At least that's what I told myself when I had stood in front of the mirror for the tenth time.

But today was not going to be like before. Gone was the easy going camaraderie, and in its place was an uncomfortable silence. He quietly filled out his report and I sat there feeling like a total idiot in my new suit.

"Hello? Is this the 'let's pretend Clare doesn't exist part of the interview' or what?"

He looked up from his report. "I'm sorry Clare. I need to get this done so I can get an early start on the road tomorrow. Big Italian thing. Unless there is some unanticipated snag, but I don't anticipate that." He actually smiled.

Unanticipated snag? I contemplated that one. Yes, there was an unanticipated snag. I started getting irritated, glancing at my watch. All the damn feds did was push their papers.

"You have any special plans for Thanksgiving?" Joe glanced up at me, continued writing.

"No."

"No? What, you sit home with a can of stew?"

"Well, it's just my brother and I, my mother's dead and my father is in Detroit." I hadn't expected to throw in the dead mother.

"Oh, I'm sorry about that. My dad is dead. Losing a parent is rough."

More scribbling.

What was I thinking anyway? I pushed the romantic possibilities from my mind and tried to stay in focus.

"Do you think this will be enough information for your superiors? I really expected a much more lengthy process, like being shuttled off to Chicago to testify in front of some type of wildlife jury."

"Oh yes, though they'll probably ask for some sort of follow up. I'm sure I'll be getting a memo on my desk in about six months asking for some sort of verification."

"It's funny that you mention it, but I've been thinking along those lines. What about holding a public meeting concerning the bear issue. We could discuss it from beginning to end. And believe me, I want to see this thing come to an end."

"That's an excellent idea. Not only does it satisfy the paperwork need, but it's good public relations for you. But you probably know everyone in town, I know how it is up here."

"Yeah I do, but it will lend me some credibility. You might find this hard to believe, but some people up here doubt my expertise. Being a woman and all." I offered up a wry smile.

"Well it's hard in this field, one of the last male strongholds, professionally speaking. My sister is in the same spot you're in, she's an assistant DA in Chicago, always getting heckled by guys for being tough. As a matter of fact, she's working on a case concerning a guy who's got ties up here, Wilfred Durant. Ever hear of him?" I shook my head. "Anyway, he's got quite a lot of land up here. I'm surprised you haven't heard of him, it's been in the papers for a while."

"No, just keeping my nose to the grindstone. I really can't say I've seen that story in the paper up here."

He chuckled. "Yeah, I suppose big city news wouldn't make it all the way up here, even with the Upper Peninsula connection. The murder was pretty grisly. She was raped and then her hands were cut off."

"Her hands?" I didn't get it. Wasn't murder enough?

He nodded. "The coroner said she bled to death, but enough said, I think I covered the gruesome quotient for the day. We're finished here." He stood up to leave. I quickly stood up also.

"Just one more thing, I'd like it very much if you could come to this public informational meeting. I was thinking of setting the date for some time after the holiday season, less hectic, and plus it will give people something to look forward to in the long winter months ahead."

"Sure. Anyway I can be of service." Snapping his briefcase shut he extended his hand in parting. He was wearing one of those waterproof watches. I thought of scuba diving.

"It has truly been a pleasure Ms. McElroy." He locked his blue eyes on mine. "I trust I'll be hearing from you then?"

I pumped his hand enthusiastically, smiling broadly and feeling indescribably silly. "Oh yes, as soon as possible." As soon as the words left my mouth I regretted it. I sounded like an eager beaver. Or smitten.

I watched him walk out the door, hoping he thought neither.

***

"Dan, really, I don't think the house needs to be dusted more than once a week." I started to chew on the end of my pen watching Dan wipe down the end table. My tiny cabin had never been so clean.

"A harmonious living space is very important. In fact, your living area reflects your state of mind. Messy dirty rooms represent mental chaos, while clean orderly rooms represent mental clarity and harmony."

He lifted the family Bible off the mantle and carefully dusted it.

"I would never expect you to display something so overtly religious. Are you a believer?"

"No."

"What? You don't believe in God?"

"No."

"Well, what do you believe in?" He plunked himself down on the couch and started leafing through the book."

"I believe that you're a royal pain in the ass, and I'm never gonna get this done if you don't leave me alone." I had let my other paperwork accumulate in lieu of my meetings with Joe. I wanted to get caught up with everything so I could begin working on our informational meeting about the bear.

"I'm just curious." He looked hurt.

"It's just something I got after mom died. Dad didn't want it anymore, so he gave it to me. Maybe he figured I'd be getting married someday and could continue on with the family history." I snorted to myself. Likely story.

I'm a believer. I think Christ had a beautiful message."

I looked over at him. He sat there glassy eyed. Transfixed by the huge Bible.

"That's great Dan, just keep it to yourself, okay?"

"You don't have to worry, I'm not that kind of Christian, I'm not a hypocrite. I just try to live the way Jesus did, that's all. Hey, did you realize these McElroys go back at least two hundred years? Someone started this all the way back in Ireland." He was peering at the name page. "We've got a long family history."

I stopped writing. Family history. It sounded strange, foreign to me. I had glanced at the Bible and its pages of dates and names, but it really didn't hold any special significance. People that were disconnected from me, strange people from a strange land. I did remember my father complaining about his 'damn old man.' I knew what he meant, I wound up feeling the same way about him. I went back to the business of writing.

"Do you plan on being at the table long?"

"Why?"

"I thought I'd do a little painting. I like to do a little every day to keep the old brush arm limber." He did an up and down stroke motion like he had a paintbrush in his hand. It reminded me of Tom Sawyer, painting a fence.

I stopped writing again and looked at my brother. It was hard for me to believe I hadn't seen him since our mother died. And there he sat on the couch, thumbing through that damn book. Somehow he appeared more sure of himself since I had seen him last, yet more fragile. Like everything he had experienced was contained within a numinous shell. He had that slightly feminine look women go wild for in a man. I tried to decide what it was. Probably the long lashes.

"Clare, I swear, you work too much," He blinked up at me. "Since I've been here you've been rushing off from one meeting to another, or working on some report, scribbling away. Why don't you go out and enjoy yourself? I here there is a guy next door who has a crush on you. Maybe you could get to know him better?" His eyes sparkled mischievously.

"Oh really? And who told you that?"

"Well Darryl, of course. He also mentioned that he didn't mean to offend you in any shape or form, he's just so, oh how did he put it? So fantastically, stupendously, attracted to you. Must be a chemistry thing. You don't feel it huh?"

"No, I don't. I'm glad to hear you have gotten so buddy buddy with Darryl. What else did he say?" Now I was curious. I hardly believed that words like fantastic or stupendous were in Darryl's vocabulary.

"He really didn't say much more about the little incident with you. He just talked a little about his past, his ex-wife. A few other people around town mentioned you though. It seems on the main your highly regarded. Although you do put people off with your standoffish manner. There are a few guys out there who definitely don't like you, but Moe, he thinks of you like a daughter. Very protective like." He nodded.

"Jesus Christ Dan! What is this bullshit? Survey my sister day? You have hardly been here a week and the whole town is talking behind my back."

He gave me a pained look. "Please don't take the Lord's name in vain."

"Oh whatever, don't give me the religious dribble, this is serious business, you might not think so, but it is. I have an image to uphold here. If these people don't respect me, forget it. I'll lose everything I've worked for. I'm an authority figure, not the friendly cop on a beat." I glared at him, hoping the words hit their mark.

He regarded me curiously. "You know something Clare? You're getting more and more like dad. That uniform and that tone of voice you use, it's uncanny. The spitting image of the old boy himself."

"Dan, if you're going to live here, you're going to have to avoid being a jerk." I stood up abruptly and walked to my room, slamming the door. His laughter rolled out after me.

"Sticks and stones! C'mon Clare, lighten up. Let's go out for a while, we can get some dinner."

I rolled over on the bed. "You go out. I want to be left alone."

"My treat."

I stared at the ceiling a minute, smiling, making him wait. "All right."

Chapter 14

I decided to spend Thanksgiving tracking down Fisher Black.

I was tying my boots up when Darryl knocked timidly on the door. He had a cornucopia wreath in his hands. Hollowed squashes and Indian corn that were strung together with grapevine. Relieved, we had embarrassingly made up.

When he left I hung it on the nail beside the door.

It was so cold the snow was like granulated sugar. I had secured the trailer and snowmobile the night before, no way was I hiking it today. Pulling out of the driveway I thought about my hunch that Fisher would be there in his cabin.

I remembered Darla saying that intuition was the basis for her decision making. She would never make the really important decisions without it. And then there was Dan, who was forever talking about the higher order, higher power, always something higher he relied on. I never quite knew what they were getting at, but thought that if you based your decisions and thought processes on your feelings, you would surely wind up in a mess. Feelings were fickle, subject to change on a moment's notice.

So what was I doing?

The trailhead was drifted over with snow. I lowered the trailer and slowly backed the snowmobile off, and quickly buzzed down the trail. I just wanted to get this done and over with.

The cabin appeared in the distance through the tree limbs. There was a light inside, and smoke was coming from the chimney. I parked the sled and got off. My hands were shaking as I undid my helmet.

Rapping quickly on the front door I took a deep breath. I'm sure he must have heard me miles away from the cabin. No one traveled this trail. They all knew where it ended.

"C'mon in, I hear ya." Fisher grumbled through the door.

I pushed on the door, and it creaked open on rusted hinges. Fisher sat glaring at me from his stool in front of the fire. His face softened as I shut the door. Whittling away at a piece of birch, I noticed he let the shavings fall to the floor. The entire floor was covered in wood shavings. He held the carving for me to see. It appeared to be a small bear.

"Now this thing…it gives me much pleasure," He turned it around in his hand.

I sat on the stool next to him and watched him work. The features of the animal were becoming more apparent. He had finished the tiny ears and the snout, and was now carving striations for the shaggy fur. Transfixed, I sat watching him carve the small bear.

The warmth from the fire was soothing, and time melted away like warm butter. Surveying the room I took in the kitchen. A small wood stove sat next to a table set for two.

He had been expecting me all along.

He glanced up at me, continued whittling.

"You know," he said, finishing up the tail, "I tried to live in your world once. The mental noise…was horrible. I was constantly buffeted by people's thoughts. People who had emotional problems, disorders, those thoughts and feelings always seemed the easiest to pick up." He grimaced. "They tore right through here," he tapped his chest. "I carried around the agony for days." He turned the carving around in his hand and I clearly saw it before it had shape, when it was a piece of wood.

"Now, it's stopped. The cyclic nature of life continues on in the woods as it has since the beginning of time. Humans aren't trying to damn up the energy or twist it to their own ends. It's very peaceful."

An unwanted memory passed behind my eyes. I saw very clearly something I had not acknowledged before; my father raising the back of his hand to my mother, my mother cowering, me protecting Dan behind a chair.

"I knew you had problems, I could sense that. I knew it when you and your friend stopped by. And I could sense it before that on the paper you left on my door."

"Paper?"

"Yes, I sensed your feelings in the paper, and on the paper,' He brushed the shavings from his pants. "The hunting license?,"

I nodded slowly in shock, realizing I was totally transparent to this man.

He laughed. "I've never used one of those, but according to you, I needed to. I had never even seen one before. A license to live from the land?" He snorted.

I looked at him indignantly. "It's for a good reason. We need kill quotas so a species won't be driven into extinction. Look, a couple hundred years ago the beaver were about driven to extinction by fur trappers, now they've rebounded because of modern management techniques." I nodded.

"That's an outward manifestation. Do people think they are on top all the time? That's the question. Everything can always take a back seat to the almighty human and this so called progress."

I felt my face get red. "Yeah, but I think people's attitudes are changing, there has been a lot of success stories. Look at the return of the California Condor, or the black footed ferret."

"Your nickel and diming everything. I'm telling you, it's the way people relate to the land." He continued to whittle.

"Regulation helps, telling people what to do, or what they can't do. What else is there?"

"Attitudes. That's what there is. People need to go inside themselves and see what they really want. The majority of people in this country are empty, always trying to fill the void with something. Power, toys—you name it. The religious, socio political, and economic systems are all interrelated, Each is reflective of the whole. That's why regulation will never work. Unless people can fuel their restless compulsion with a reality other than our current paradigm provides…the Earth will be eaten alive."

I sat for a few minutes and digested this. My stomach started to rumble.

"That's all very nice for you but I've got to find my way in the real world."

He handed me the carving.

"For me?"

He nodded. I turned it around in my hand. It was perfect.

"So now what?"

He scratched his chin. "Let's eat."

Chapter 15

The house was full of Delmatos, Rigones, Parettis and Ablemans. Joe gazed at his many relations milling about, he was about to nod off. The endless rounds of red wine and the smorgasbord of old favorites had about done him in. He turned towards the table, wondered about getting some coffee. It was funny how the American turkey sat as the centerpiece surrounded by a sea of foreign dishes.

Pheeny plopped down in a plush velvet chair beside him. Mama's expensive mahogany chairs for the holidays. Joe couldn't remember a time when he hadn't seen these chairs.

"So how's it goin' Joey?" She tweaked his ear.

"Ow. Stop it. I'm tired."

"Tired, smired." She poured herself some wine from one of the bottles on the table.

"Will you take a look at Aunt Regine? What is her problem? Sixty years old and trying to flirt with every new guy that comes to these Thanksgiving dinners." Pheeny narrowed her eyes over the top of her wine glass and peered at Aunt Regine. She was dressed in a very low cut shimmery blouse and a too tight mini skirt. Every Thanksgiving Aunt Regine had made it a habit to come on to one of the cousin's boyfriends, flirting with him unmercifully. Joe felt it was interesting to watch the cousins reactions.

"Why is it we're the couple without a couple. We are coupleless." Pheeny hiccuped and turned her attention back to Joe.

"I don't know, maybe it's 'cause we don't want to tangle with the likes of Aunt Regine," He yawned, rubbing his eyes. "Actually, there is somebody."

"Somebody?" Pheeny widened her eyes. "Who is she anyway?"

"Oh just a woman I met on a case I've been investigating. She seems lonely."

"So what's this, a charity case? Believe me Joe, you don't want to get involved with someone to fix them."

"I didn't mean like that. What I meant is that maybe she could be interested, maybe there isn't anyone in her life."

"Oh. Well, what's she like?"

"I don't know. I like her, she's intelligent, attractive." Joe ran his fingers through his hair, trying to reconstruct Clare in his mind. He thought of the Upper Peninsula of Michigan in its quiet blanket of snow, contrasted it with the grayness of Chicago.

"It wouldn't work anyway. She lives in Michigan, I live here. Just a fantasy."

"A fantasy huh? I haven't heard you mention anyone at all Joe, not in a long time. Why don't you pursue this? Have some fun in your life."

"Yeah, fun," He sighed. "What about you? Life in the fast lane with all those boyfriends, how many are you trying to choose from now?"

Pheeny gave a tight, little laugh. "Yeah, well I give up. I've about had it with the dating scene. Remember that WASP guy I was dating? What a blue blood."

She gulped some wine at the memory, flooding her throat with the warmth of forgetting, before the memory became a torrent of anger. The memory of him and herself. She knew then he had labeled her, her and all exotic looking women as the *other*. She shook her head slowly at the frozen memory.

Joe watched her face, then put an arm around her. "Hey…You all right?"

She sniffed into her hand.

"Why don't you date someone more like yourself, someone you have more in common with? These guys you've seen, they're nothing like you."

"What in the hell do you mean like me? Italian and Catholic, is that what you mean? Male chauvinist pigs. Yeah, that's what I need." Her eyes were blazing.

A picture of the the pope hung on the wall in front of them. Joe figured he was lucky. He never had to worry about woman trouble.

"No, that is not what I mean. There seems to be a mix-up in the communication today sis. Maybe it's you and the wine."

Pheeny raised her wine glass in toast.

"What I mean is someone down to earth. Someone who is good, kind, and hard working. You know what I mean?"

"I have my career to think about; I don't want to settle down to a bunch of kids. She sniffed in contempt. "Sure, that's what I got a law degree for, to play second fiddle to some guy, wiping some snot nose kids. Forget it." She impatiently drummed her fingers on the table.

"C'mon. Your lonely, admit it. Isn't that what this is all about? Both of us getting up there in age, wanting someone special?"

"Jesus, Joe, you sound like ma. She must have got to you."

Joe considered. Pheeny was angry, nothing to do but wait it out. "Anyway, how is that case you've been working on turning out, the one with the murdered woman?"

"Which one?"

"The suspect that has ties to the U.P."

"Oh that," She sighed, then brightened. "I did meet a reporter who wants to help on the case. He's very big on feminism. Can you imagine?"

He was happy he snapped her out of her funk so quickly. "Maybe things will fall into place fairly quickly now. The case could be solved in no time."

"I wouldn't count on it."

He glanced over and saw that her face had clouded again.

Chapter 16

Dan kept glancing towards Moe at the bar, obviously to get the go ahead that it was okay to be sitting with us because we were drinking. I was getting irritated with the whole thing, Dan had been coming here to paint, and it seemed I could never get away from him. If he wasn't home he was in the tavern painting. He had painted the inside of the bar, and the outside façade. He had painted the view of the lake. He had painted the lake complete with all manner of wildlife taking an evening drink. The list went on and on.

People were fascinated with the new resident artist and I knew Dan was sorely in need of an ego boost. Having drifted in and out of reality his entire life. He now found people paying two to three hundred dollars for his paintings. Personally I found it ironic people would spend so much time in a bar then go home to a picture of it on their wall. But I suppose art reflected life.

He said he was saving to buy a studio in the spring and I was peeved. All this money was rolling in, and he hadn't offered to pay any rent yet.

"A toast to Dan and his new found artistic success." Darla smiled at Dan and everyone at our table raised their glasses. A few patrons at nearby tables smiled and nodded in our direction. For some reason this only increased my irritation.

"With all this new found wealth, maybe you can help with your share of the rent?"

"Rent? Oh, sure, can't we talk about this at home?"
Dan looked stricken.

"I never see you at home, you're always here." I
glared at him over the top of my glass.

"Well…" He threw up his hands in supplication,
got up and went over to the bar. I watched him as he
walked, hands in pockets, hunched over.

"Man, Clare, why are you so mean to the guy? He
hasn't been here that long. It sounds like he's been
through a lot." Darla peered at me as she pushed her
glasses on top of her head.

"He needs some toughening up, time to get a reality
check," I set my beer on the coaster. "Don't get me
wrong, of course I'm happy for him. He just needs to
pull his weight, not meander in artistic la-la land. The
world doesn't revolve around Dan."

"No, of course not. But right now he is White
Cloud's celebrity. Don't you think Darryl?"

"I guess he has been spending a lot of time here,"
Darryl scratched his head thoughtfully. "I've been
thinking I'd get him to help around the farm, with Smith
and Wesson and the sleigh. It's that time of year."

I nodded in agreement. "That would do him some
good. Ground him. Get him out on the land, give him a
sense of duty, of community."

"Speaking of community, what about your public
forum? How's that shaping up?' Darla perked up.

"Uh, slow." I slouched in my seat. So far I had
pushed some papers around. Some ideas.

"Have you called the fish and wildlife guy?"

"No."

"Oh…Well, it's just not like you. You're usually so
prompt, attending to detail and all."

"I tell you what people are going to say," Darryl
piped in, "They're going to say, so what? That kid wasn't

one of ours, it was a tourist, a Fudgie." He nodded, as if we should congenially acknowledge this fact.

"So what are you saying Darryl? I shouldn't even bother?"

"Well...I don't think it will do any good. People know about bears around here, we keep the population in check. We hunt. You know that."

"Yeah, but do people around here know about the connection between bear problems and human encroachment? I don't think so." said Darla.

"I would have to agree with her, though I understand your point. Tourists can get lazy about leaving food out if they don't understand the opportunism of the bears. Yes, people around here understand the up and down of the bear population, you kill a bear and there's one less bear, but do they understand things like habitat depredation, lack of adequate home ranges for males, that type of thing? I don't think so. We have a great resource around here, I'd like to see people protect it by learning how to be educated stewards."

"Well spoken Clare."

We looked at Darryl.

"All right you two. Enough is enough. I can't win with the both of you." Grimacing, Darryl swigged from his bottle of Bud.

Dan sauntered back to the table.

"Hey you guys, still got a spot for me?"

"Sure." Darla scooched over.

"Damn right Dan, sit right down. I need some defense from these irate women. They've been insulting my intelligence again, picking apart my opinions and basically trying to corner me into saying I'm a stupid idiot."

Dan looked uncomfortable. "I don't want to get in the way of your argument. I just walked away from one.

I'm trying to become more peaceful. Would anyone like to accompany me to the quote, unquote, rez? Moe suggested a meeting there."

Darla laughed. "An AA meeting? Traditional or non?"

Dan looked confused.

"What I mean is, Christian or traditional Indian?"

"Oh. Well, I guess it's Christian, that being my religious affiliation."

"Which one would you go to Clare?" Darla slyly glanced at me.

"Neither." I shifted uneasily in my seat.

"So you see yourself as fitting into neither camp, traditional or non?"

"Well no, Darla, I'm not an Indian."

"Yes, but you would agree that there is a traditional way and a western way of viewing the world?"

"I suppose there's many ways of viewing the world, and I choose to subscribe to neither camp, thank-you." I ruffled my hair, feeling agitated.

Darla rolled her eyes at me. "Sooner or later you have to pick a guiding force in your life."

"Okay, I have picked a unifying vision. The scientific one. Non-mystical, very simple."

"That's not a philosophy, or a moral code. All it tells you is that two and two make four."

"Actually, I think when you have two, and get two more, you know you've got four, so you feel good about that. You know what to expect. Very clear way of operating in the world."

Darla shook her head impatiently at me. "No, you're not getting it. That's not what I'm saying."

"Can you be a little more specific then? I don't understand these insinuations." My voice was rising in volume.

She set her mouth in a firm line and studied my face. "What I'm trying to get at is if you have a certain way of viewing the world, a set of values to guide your life by. Science can't guide your life."

I frowned at her. "Of course I have values. Most people know right from wrong."

She was shaking her head again. "No, no, no. I give up. I guess what I was, am, trying to do is see what angle you're coming from. What starting point do you begin your path from? What—"

"All right already. I think I'm getting the picture. I would have thought you had figured it out by now, the way Dan is always haranguing me about church. I don't have any religious affiliation. There, satisfied?"

"No."

"People are always talking about this camp, the other camp, you know, dividing lines. I think Clare's in the hard working camp. She'll always do the right thing." Darryl quickly nodded at me.

"Yeah, we'll see. Talk to you guys later," She flipped some bills on the table. "Oh and Dan, congratulations on everything you've put together for yourself here. You really do have quite a talent." She patted his back on her way out.

After she left the three of us sat there.

"Well," I started abruptly, "I guess that's that."

"No," Dan was staring out the window. "I don't think it is."

***

The smell of bacon and pancakes drifted through the air as I floated towards the sea of wakefulness. Grabbing snatches of dream fragments as they drifted past me, I snuggled deeper into the covers. Dan was whistling in the kitchen. I groaned, turning over.

It was a sound I had heard a long time ago; the clatter off dishes, the smell of a Sunday morning. The familiarity of it all flooded me. It seemed so simple.

Maybe Darla was right. Maybe I was being too much of a hard-ass.

Yawning, I rolled out of bed and rubbed the back of my neck. What I longed for was a deep smooth sleep. Like dark chocolate. Undisturbed by dreams of bears.

I shuffled out to the kitchen. Pouring myself a cup of coffee, I sat down at the table, watching Dan. He looked over at me, flipping pancakes..

"Hey, good morning,"

"Hey." I mumbled, sticking my nose in my coffee mug.

"You're favorite, blueberry pancakes."

I managed a smile. The blueberries reminded me of Kyle. We had foraged together in August at an abandoned blueberry farm not far from here. I think he had stuck more in his mouth then in the bucket.

"Yeah, they are my favorite. And if you don't mind, you can whip up a batch of blueberry syrup to go with the pancakes."

Smiling mischievously he sat opposite me, plunking down some maple syrup.

"This will have to do."

"Oh."

"In more ways than one."

"Oh?"

"Yeah, we don't have cinnamon rolls. No, really I want to say I'm sorry about the whole rent thing. I think I should have brought it up in the beginning. Also, I don't know exactly what it is, how to put my finger on it, but I feel like you are really unhappy with me somehow. You seem angry all the time Clare. Why can't you just take me how I am? I'm taking little baby steps, that's all I can do."

I raised my eyebrows while stuffing pancakes in my mouth. Chewing vigorously I swallowed. "Yeah, you're right. I am mad."

"Why?"

"Because you show up on my doorstep expecting me to welcome you with open arms after how you have lied and cheated me in the past. *Stole* from me Dan. Trust comes slowly. If at all."

He frowned. "I know Clare, I know. What can I tell you? I won't do it again? All I can do is tell you that I take it one day at a time. That's my path."

"Let's hope your path doesn't lead you astray."

We lapsed into silence, our forks clinking against the plates. I began to get uncomfortable.

"Look, just pay me one hundred dollars a month and we'll call it even. That should give you enough left over for this studio your saving for."

"Fine. That sounds fair. As long as you're comfortable with that decision." He looked at me. "Are you?"

"Yes, of course I am. That's why I said it."

He watched me eat for a minute. "Do you remember playing in the rain as kids? How we loved to go out and just run? We used to get soaked."

"Not really." I pushed my plate away and poured myself some more coffee.

"I remember a light rain slowly starting, and we'd will it to rain harder. If we had our wish it would just pour, the sky would literally open up and rain cats and dogs. We'd be drenched to the bone splashing in those puddles. Mom would always yell for us to come in if it started lightening though."

"If she wasn't passed out." I said frowning.

Dan bit his lip remembering. "She passed out quite a bit, and you took care of me after that." He was silent for a moment. I brushed crumbs from the table and into the cup of my hand, trying not to think of rain.

"Apart from the freedom of running in the rain, I remember the worms."

"The worms?"

He nodded. "How they would come up from the ground and make their way over to the sidewalk where they would twist and turn in the water, finally getting still. It used to break your heart, you would cry and cry, picking worms off the sidewalk and putting them back in the grass. Of course they would drown in the soil, that's exactly what they were trying to get away from, but you didn't know that back then. I remember watching you, terrified that my sister was crying over worms." He shook his head at the memory.

My eyes moved restlessly around the cabin, looking for something to settle on. I felt a cringe of agitation at the nape of my neck. I got up from the table and went into the kitchen, started washing the dishes.

"Oh Dan, I don't remember that, I was just a kid, what, five, six years old? We did a lot of goofy things."

"I remember feeling what you were feeling, Clare. You felt the worms suffering, their loss and their anguish. Their dying. And there wasn't much you could do about it."

"Well, I'm sure I wasn't up to making sound judgements about worms at the age of five." I snapped at him, unintentionally, but the conversation was making me edgy.

Dan eyed me cautiously. "The point being, that it's a good memory, and I'm glad I shared it with you. Looking back on it, it taught me a lesson about life."

"Worms? About life?"

"It's important to feel other creatures pain, to empathize with them, that somehow we're all related."

I laughed. "Well, Dan, that's a nice story, but in my profession worms are bait."

Wiping my hands on the dish towel I strung it through the fridge handle. Then I walked outside to gather firewood in the cold morning air.

Chapter 17

Durant drove down Lakeshore Drive in the late afternoon sunshine, skyscrapers reflected in his dark glasses. The warm glow of the sun illuminated his face while he caressed his chin feeling the stubble of five o'clock shadow. He glanced in the mirror at his reflection, smiled, as the hidden eyes stared back, frozen like beetles.

Today was an exceptional day. Not only had he made a killing on two extremely large and perfectly prime lakeshore properties, he had fired that crazy bitch in the main office. She had been coming in bleary eyed to the office, complaining, no whining really, about a sick kid at home. Today she had accidentally put a call directly through to his office, rather than letting his personal secretary screen it. That was it. He had coolly and calmly went up to the front and told her to pack her shit, she was out.

Durant was happy to humiliate her. Teach everyone else a lesson. Smug, he had walked out of the office into the crisp sunshine.

Relishing his triumph he thought about it; more land, and one less crazy bitch in the office. He shoved the gear in fourth, bypassing three lanes of traffic. Smoothing out way ahead, he curved into the lane for his turnoff.

The estate was set far back from the road on the lake. He paused at the entrance and ran his security code. The wrought iron gate opened.

Having an exquisite sense of taste and style, the elements in his surroundings were perfectly harmonized. His fondness of gardening and cooking had also grown appreciably. Looking forward to preparing a meal while sipping a glass of wine, Durant opened the door.

Monique was there to greet him. She had learned to anticipate when he would be home. It was a sixth sense that served her well, and Durant expected it. He had come across her in a gentleman's club, and had quickly and discreetly notified the domestic service that there was a need for her services. She had arrived two days later with a modest size bag. It was everything she owned.

She was everything that he had sought in a maid. Skilled in the domestic arts, she had made his castles into pleasant homes. A home was a bastion, a fortress against the outside world in which he increasingly delved. Here he was no longer bothered by outside pressures. Monique and the other domestics would see to that.

But perhaps today would be different. He sensed an air of unease around Monique. Her blond hair was pulled casually back in a ponytail, the makeup was impeccable. He couldn't quite place the unrest, but sniffed it out nevertheless.

"Sir?" She began tentatively.

"Yes?" Durant responded in a cordial, yet controlled way.

Monique was breathing heavily, obviously distraught. Durant found himself increasingly agitated and aroused. He placed his hands on her shoulders.

"Tell me. What is it?" His eyes bore into hers.

"Sir, Josephine Delmato has been calling the house, wanting to speak to you. There is also some sort of legal notification on the table in the foyer. I'm sorry sir, I didn't know what to do. I told her you would be gone for at least a week. She told me to have you contact her as soon as possible."

"Legal notification?" Durant again spoke in the same controlled voice. He briskly walked to the foyer and picked up the letter. He then proceeded to the study. Loosening his tie as he went, he shut the door behind him. A bitter smile crept over his face as he read.

Chapter 18

Pheeny was on the floor, laughing hysterically over a story about a farmer who had a pig he regularly took for a walk, and how the pig had escaped. All she could think of was the pig running down the road away from the farmer, looking over his shoulder to see if the farmer was still coming after him.

"A huge pig!" She howled.

Cole watched her with a serious expression on his face.

"Oh yeah, I was there when it happened, pig running down the road and all. Huge pig. The farmer didn't think anything of it. He said he ran away all the time. He would run a while, so as not to lose sight of the pig, and I would have to run to try to keep up with him. I was glad I had been running two days a week at that point." Cole nodded in retrospect, sipping his wine.

The remains of a large pizza lay before them. They had decided to have a brain storming session at her place. She had thought that a pizza and a bottle of merlot would be good for them. Relax the brain muscles. Now the paper plates and pizza crusts littered the floor, the bottle of wine was almost finished.

Pheeny rubbed her eyes and tried to catch her breath. Jinkies the cat stepped through the door, and with an air of haughtiness surveyed the scene. He looked around curiously and sniffed at a pizza crust.

"Hey Jinkies, c'mere boy. You must think I'm a nut, rolling around uncontrollably." She rubbed behind his ears affectionately.

"Jinkies? Where have I heard that before?"

"Thelma always said that in exclamation on *Scooby Doo*. You must remember that cartoon. He was always so wide eyed as a kitten, he just looked like a Jinkies." Pheeny smiled.

Cole nestled further into the camel chair. He surveyed the wall. Joe's photographs of the Upper Peninsula hung in a series of five, Lake Superior hung in the middle, surrounded by a close-up of leaves and a forest in fall foliage. A moose and a bear hung on either end, rounding out the series.

"These photographs of your brother's are really good. I'm assuming it's your brother, right? Maybe I can convince him to partner with me on a feature article."

Pheeny glanced over. "Yeah, those are Joe's. I used to get one or two a year, now I'm supposed to be content with socks." She shook her head.

"You don't like socks?"

"Oh I don't know. I suppose the reality of life rears up and smacks me in the face. Joe and I used to be much closer, more optimistic. More idealistic about life and our goals. Joe is on his way to becoming an entrenched bureaucrat, and me, well, I guess I have to realize I can't catch all the bad guys." She frowned.

Cole saw the tension in her face. "I think, Ms Delmato, you need a vacation. Time off to get some perspective on things. It sounds like you're getting a heavy case of burnout."

"Nah, I can't take time off yet. We're getting a lot closer, I can smell it. In a few weeks I'll have enough to pull him in for good, lock him up."

"I thought you were presumed innocent until proven guilty? Don't obsess about it Josephine. It will come when it's ready."

"Whose side are you on anyway?"

"All right, listen to this idea, it just came to me. Let's go to the UP where this guy has some supposed business dealings. You know Dee Dee was from there?"

She nodded.

"We can do a little investigative reporting, and I'll show you what it's like on the other side of the newspaper. Plus, we get the added benefit of being in beautiful county, it's great up there, you'll love —"

"I know, I know, my brother worked up there, remember? I've been up there a few times, and yes, it is beautiful. Maybe a little harsh this time of year though."

"Like Chicago isn't? That's what fireplaces are for. So what do you say? My proposition is this; a little R and R, and a little work. Come on." He gave her a playful push with his hand.

"Well.."

"Think of the pasties, smoked fish."

"All right already! Let's go."

***

They crossed the Mackinaw bridge around sunset, the orange sun melted into blue. Pheeny watched as the colors converged and swallowed each other in the vastness of sky and water.

"This bridge is huge." She gazed up at the supporting scaffolding.

"It is," Cole agreed. "I believe it's about five miles across, and who knows how far down." He inched the car closer to the side, glancing down.

"Jesus Cole! What are you trying to do, kill us?"

109

Laughing, Cole switched lanes, passing a logging truck. "Did you know people come up here to commit suicide? Last year a guy drove up here from down state, stopped at the first pillar, and jumped right off. People said he didn't even hesitate."

She shivered looking down. The dark water continually churned topped by icy white caps. The bridge was the place that Lake Michigan met Lake Huron. Pheeny could barely make out Mackinaw Island to the east, a dark blob on the water.

"My comment to that would be you are a veritable sea of information Detective Cole."

"We used to come up here every summer vacation. My mom was a school teacher, so she of course had the summers off."

"I see," Pheeny looked straight ahead, she was relieved to see they were heading down the bridge towards the toll booth.

"Like I mentioned before, my brother Joe worked up here, or should I say played in the woods doing God knows what." She paused remembering. "I guess I shouldn't be so flip, he was working on an eagle project. I'm trying to remember where it was at," She furrowed her brow in concentration. "What I remember was the forest. Never in my life have I seen so many trees. Trees upon trees upon trees."

"That's what a forest is."

"Smart ass. What I'm trying to convey here is the overwhelming sense I had of being so far from civilization. They only had a little dinky dirt road up to their cabin. Joe called it a two track. You just had the feeling of being cut off from everything. But I liked it. I liked the quite, the serenity of the place, and yes, the trees. The views were spectacular. I remember Joe and I took a long hike to the top of this peak, and you could see forever."

"You must have been in the Porkies then."

"Yes, that was it, the Porkies. Short for the Porcupine Mountains. Pheeny nodded remembering.

"A dollar fifty sir." Cole handed the money to the woman in the booth.

"Here we are, on the other side of the bridge, in the U.P." He took out a map from the side of the door. Flipping it open, he kept one hand on the wheel. "Can you steer while I look at this thing?"

"Oh no, I'm not going to steer. Let me look at the map while you concentrate on driving the car. I can see you're a major risk taker, first veering off on the bridge, and now trying to read maps and drive at the same time." Pheeny snatched the map from his lap.

"All right, where are we going?"

"A little place called White Cloud."

"White Cloud? Sounds familiar. Why does that name sound familiar?"

"I don't know."

She traced her finger along highway two, running along Lake Michigan. She glanced up at the signs bearing down on them.

"Take the route along the lake here on highway two. We have a ways to go." Pheeny settled back in her seat. She carefully folded the map and placed it next to her.

"Well sweet mama justice, we're no longer traveling blind." Cole glanced over at her, grinning.

"What are you talking about, sweet mama justice? I don't know if I like the sound of that."

"You know, justice is blind? It's a joke."

"Anyone or anything that has alluded to the fact that the scales of justice are blind is full of it. Justice can think, see, and hear. Justice is also full of opinions."

She started picking puffballs off of her wool coat, annoyed at her once naïve state of mind. "Anyway, sweet mama is rather derogatory. Sounds sexist."

"Oh no. Sweet mama is what you are. You're sweet and passionate to do what's right. That's what I like about you. Being so fiery and all."

"Oh. I see. And here I thought you were some reporter out to make a name for himself."

Cole frowned. "Well if I look at myself totally objectively, which is very hard to do, maybe that's not entirely untrue. I operate on hunches, you know, a nose for news. It's gotten me the same place your passion has, that and the fact that my sister was raped by some loser from hell, who transferred hell over to her."

Pheeny looked over at him, his face had grown hard. Cole gripped the steering wheel and stared straight ahead.

She was silent for a moment. "I'm sorry."

"It's done, over. Now she has to deal with all the psychological effects. What a load I tell you. Therapy for a few years, some serious antidepressants…her whole family has been affected. She's married with two kids." He glanced at Pheeny, then looked out the window at the gathering night.

The sun was long gone. Remnants of the disappearing colors bled lightly into one another. An orange gray hue lay like oil on the water. Pheeny watched the water and mulled it over in her mind, sensing that he wasn't quite finished saying what he had to say.

"Hopefully he was put behind bars?" She asked tentatively.

"Just for a few months. My sister was one of the brave ones to actually go to court with her rape. You know how it is, so many women are ashamed and embarrassed to take the case to court, like somehow they provoked or deserved it."

Pheeny nodded. She had seen too many cases like that: the woman broken, left to piece her life back together, shrinking from the dark, from parked cars. From everything.

"You know what?," she said, "we can rectify a little wrong in the world by this case we're working on. That at least makes me happy."

"I hope so." Cole turned on the radio. Bob Seger was strumming about his night moves.

The lights of a town began to flicker in the distance, making Pheeny think of dying stars.

Chapter 19

Dan had gotten in the habit of going over to Moe's house in the morning before he opened the tavern, they would then attend an AA meeting at the church in town. The meetings were held in the basement of the building. Dan had complained that the coffee was too weak, but it was the best meeting around. The sunshine group, they called themselves.

Ironic name, I thought, for alcoholics in the U.P. during the dead of winter.

I had decided to go to the field office when Dan showed no signs of leaving. He said that it was strange I was leaving for the office since I had mentioned that he was never home. He argued that I was sending him mixed messages.

I told him I was a creature of habit and worked better alone.

The road curved along the Sturgeon River. Spruce and hemlock covered the view of the river most of the way, but the trees opened up to two large marshes in quick succession of one another. Now they lay frozen over in white.

I looked forward to the spring, when the marsh was alive and singing with birds. Every male redwing blackbird would be on top of a cattail about ten feet apart from the other males. There was constant chaos. When one would fly to close, the other would charge. In the pursuit of mates, everyone wanted his prime spot.

Then the great blue herons would appear. They came in the spring to fish, having a rookery near here. It looked like an impossible feat for birds so big and gangly to nest in trees. I always wondered why nature didn't design them to nest on the ground, folding up their long legs neatly underneath them. But they all flew amongst themselves in a great raucous mass of wings and legs, dangling towards their own separate nests in the rookery.

Nature provided safety in numbers. Many eyes peering for predators.

I rounded the bend to the office thinking of eyes.

Many things to do and only one of me. Sighing, I threw the gear in park and jumped out of the truck. I noticed that Hank's truck was gone.

Hank was an excellent technician. I rarely had to tell him what to do, he was efficient, and organized his time well. It was easy to like him and that surprised me. I thought it would take a while to get over Dale being fired, but I just couldn't hold a grudge against Hank.

I unlocked the front door, and stepped inside. The place smelled of old books and stuffed specimens. Strange, unless you were a biologist.

The place was like part lab and part old forgotten library. Bottles of collected specimens filled the tables lining all four walls. Some were dry, and some were in formaldehyde. But all were neatly arranged in alphabetical order. Everything that resided in a northern Michigan forest was bottled or stuffed in this office. Or, if I couldn't find it in a bottle, the bookshelves above the tables contained an impressive array of scientific works. I had everything from atmosphere to zoology at my fingertips.

Turning away from the books and specimens I walked over to my desk. The desks were situated at the far wall, devoid of samples or books. Hank had asked to stick a bookshelf between the two desks, complaining of feeling my eyes boring into him when he was sitting there doing paperwork. I laughed, telling him I didn't care if he did, just as long as he filled it with something other than science books. He had proceeded to fill it with his accumulated collection of animal skulls. Through his work along stream banks, old fields, and hardwood forests, Hank had managed to find representatives of most every genus that inhabited these northern climes. I was amazed at this knack of his for finding dead and decayed things. He even beat out my keen observational skills.

"Clare, youse might be a nature cop, but youse don't have the Yooper blood." Hank had winked at me, exaggerating the thick, Yooper accent of the old-timers. He had been holding a bear skull, his latest find.

I stood staring at it now, remembering how Hank had once put a pipe in its jaw and a straw hat on its cranium. It seemed unnatural, and I told him to take the stuff off. I had been uncomfortable catching it in the corner of my eye. Mocking me.

I picked up the skull and brought it back to the desk, throwing my coat over the chair. Hank had left me a note on all the bear sightings in the area.

From quickly scanning the memo it appeared that our 'bear hotline' was gaining in popularity. We were hoping to radio collar a few likely males and keep an eye on them.

I quickly ran through the list. Edna Muscotti had seen a sow and cubs rummaging through the trash heap in her back yard; I crossed this one out. Rudolf Kates had a bear follow him through the woods when he was hunting for coyotes; George McDaniels had seen two bears ambling down a utility right of way corridor.-I laughed at this one, "ambling" was not a word Hank would use. He must have copied it verbatim from George.

A frantic knock at the door made me jump, scattering my thoughts like leaves on the wind. Usually people walked right in if they saw a truck outside. Someone was probably lost and needed directions.

"Come in!" I waited, then walked over to the door and opened it. There stood Kyle with a young badger in his arms.

"What in the—" I realized he had been crying. Why he wasn't in school could wait.

"Come on." I quickly ushered him in, closing the door against the blowing cold "See you found a friend."

He nodded.

"Did it bight you?"

He shook his head no. It figured. Kyle had a way with animals.

"Let's bring it over to the desk."

I wasn't keen on having this terrified creature poop all over my desk, but there was no other place to it. My predecessors had neglected to make office accommodations for wounded wildlife.

He lay the badger down carefully, looking relieved that I was in charge.

Donning my thickest gloves I sat in the chair to examine the animal. It weakly hissed at me, leaving its mouth half open.

"Clare is going to make you all better now." He spook soothingly.

The animal opened one eye and glared at me with all it had, which didn't look like much. It looked like he had been down a while.

"Kyle look," I said. "Mr. badger here has a very hurt leg. I'm going to do what I can, but he may just be too far gone to make it." I quick glanced over at him. His face was frozen.

"Okay, I want you to hold him down while I go get some medicine and a splint for his broken leg."

I went to the fridge in the corner expecting to find nothing inside, but found myself silently praising Hank for being so efficient, he had placed an early order for the ketamine hydrochloride.

Grabbing two syringes from the drawer, I drew up the anesthetic and a broad spectrum antibiotic. When I turned around the badger was on the floor.

"Clare, look! The badger is better!"

"Yeah. I see that." At least I had drew up a dose of the ketamine. "Looks like I'm going to have to grab him real quick. Here badger, badger," I crooned, walking over slowly. "Kyle, don't move." I warned.

I circled around the creature and deftly picked him up by the back of his neck, bringing him over to the desk again.

"Quick Kyle, grab a pair of those leather gloves on the shelf over there and hold him down. I don't think he's going to be so mellow anymore."

Kyle did as he was told and grabbed the animal, pinning it to the desk as I gave the shots in quick succession.

"Whoa! That was a close call." I started to breath again.

"So what do you expect to do with this guy?"

"Keep him in the barn. His name's Mr. Pepper."

"Okay then, Mr. Pepper, I'm sorry to tell you that you'll need medical attention while your leg heals."

"I know that."

I was silent for a minute. "It's nature's way of getting rid of the sick and wounded. Wild animals don't go to the doctor like people do. If you didn't come along, this guy would be dead."

"But I took Mr. Pepper to you, and you fixed him because you're a doctor. An animal doctor." He stroked the badger's fur.

I debated the logic of talking about survival of the fittest with a six year old. "Sometimes animals get sick or hurt and they die. Just like people."

"Aren't people animals? They told us in school people are animals." He looked up at me.

"Well people are special animals," I said. "They can do things other animals can't."

"Other animals can do things you can't. You can't run as fast as Smith or Wesson."

"That's true. But I can write, read, and think about things that Smith and Wesson can't think about."

"You don't know what Smith and Wesson think about."

"Yeah, you're right," I conceded. "People are just big, dumb animals too."

He frowned at me. "People aren't dumb. Well...most people aren't dumb."

"Oh? So maybe a few people are dumb?"

"Yes."

"Like who?"

"Billy Creighton. He picks his boogers and puts them under the desk." He rolled his eyes and shook his head.

"Yeah. That is kind of dumb." I said smiling.

"It sure is. But I guess it's better than eating them in front of everybody."

I laughed. "That definitely is a private matter. And you know what?"

"What?"

"Here's one thing we can agree on. This badger is fixed."

"Yeah." Kyle breathed a sigh of relief, gazing down at the anesthetized badger on my desk.

"An early present to you kid. Merry Christmas."

***

We bumped along the road and I feared the badger would come too. I had pulled a medium size animal cage out of storage and put him in it. He was still groggy with his tongue lolling out of his mouth. Occasionally he would lick his gums, eyes trying to focus. Kyle seemed unconcerned, he was staring straight ahead.

"I can take you either to school or home, which would you prefer?"

He sat quietly, staring straight ahead.

"Kyle, did you hear me?"

"Yeah." He looked out the window, keeping his face away from me.

"What's wrong?"

"Nothing."

"It's something, not nothing. You know your dad won't exactly be happy that your bringing Mr. Pepper home, that and the fact your missing school. Well look," I glanced at my watch. "We could all eat lunch up at your house. Your dad should be taking a lunch break from plowing the roads."

"No! I don't want too." He shifted uncomfortably in his seat, obviously agitated.

"You're just going to have to face the music sooner or later." I said.

Kyle looked over at me. "My dad hates me, I don't want to go home. Ever." He started crying, breaking into great, wracking sobs.

"Jesus Kyle." I pulled the truck over to the side of the road, narrowly missing the snow covered ditch. I pulled him over to me, snot and tears running all over my arm.

"Hey, hey," I stroked his hair. "Your dad doesn't hate you, he gets busy, a little frustrated, but I know he doesn't hate you. He loves you. I know sometimes he yells…" I didn't know what else to add. Goddamn it Darryl, I thought grimly, I need to have a little talk with you.

He breathed in a great gulp of air.

I held him away from me and examined his tear stained face. "You feel better now?" He nodded tiredly, snuffling and running his hand over his nose.

"Poor kid," I said pulling him close again. "Listen, I'll take you to school first, then drop Mr. Pepper off. After that I'll break the news to your dad. Does that sound like a good idea?"

He nodded his head against me, then pulled away over to his side of the seat. I looked at him for a few seconds. He looked absolutely miserable, like he was carrying the weight of the world on his shoulders.

"Okay," He mumbled. "Let's just go."

I started the truck and pulled out onto the road. We drove in silence.

I dejectedly wondered what the hell was wrong. Darryl wasn't the best of dads, but he was all right. Passable. I knew his mother was gone and he never saw her. But no one had ever mentioned why.

The part that bothered me the most was that Kyle was so damn unhappy. No child should be so depressed.

I angrily threw the gear in park when we arrived at the school. He jumped.

"I'm sorry, I guess I'm a little upset myself right now."

He looked at me wide eyed. "At me? Please don't be mad at me." His face contorted, getting ready to cry again.

"No, no," I chortled a tight little laugh, tousling his hair. "I'm not mad at you. I know this is hard for you to understand, but I'm mad at the situation. Not you."

He opened the door and got out. I watched as he walked up to the big, heavy doors of the school and pulled one open. He looked so small compared to those doors.

My mind wandered back to when I was a kid, and the fear I felt facing my father's wrath. All doors seemed so big back then. So big. Who knew what was on the other side? I shook the thought off, sighing.

I looked down at the badger. He was eyeing me glumly.

"All right listen, any trouble from you and you get a little shot. Understand? Euthanzied." I drew a finger under my throat. The badger looked up at me with black eyes, seemingly disinterested with what I had to say.

I drove slowly towards the direction of home, thinking about Kyle. He was such a sensitive kid. Always caring for hurt animals, even insects. I remembered him gingerly picking a monarch butterfly off the driveway and flicking dirt off its crumpled wings. Trying to get it to fly. I contrasted this image with Darryl and snorted.

I summed it up thinking he must have had a good mother. A kind mother

And now I was stuck with an injured badger.

My life was getting too complicated. I just wanted to go back to my cabin and take a nap.

What was I doing here anyway? Maybe it was time to move further away. Far away from people and all of their assorted problems they kept trying their damnedest to get me involved in.

Pulling into the drive, I noticed Darryl's truck parked out back. I got out of the truck and walked up the few steps to the back door. Darryl was sitting at the kitchen table reading the paper.

Taking a deep breath I knocked on the door. Darryl looked up, surprised.

"Clare! What are you doing here? C'mon in." He held the door open as I walked inside.

Shivering, I stomped my boots on the entrance way carpet.

"Sit down, sit down," He nodded his head towards a chair. "Do you want any coffee? I just made a pot. I always make more than I need."

"That would be good."

"So what's up? You never come over for lunch," He sat down and looked at me expectantly. "Staying busy nature cop? Making the world safe for hunters and fishermen?"

"Yeah well, today was kind of slow. I had a kid, Kyle, that is, come to the office with a wounded juvenile badger." I thought I would ease my way into this.

"What? Kyle took a badger to your office? How in the hell did he get there? Jesus, that office is half an hour from here!"

"He said Mrs. Bertram brought him out. Apparently Kyle convinced her that I have some kind of expertise in doctoring wounded wildlife."

"Jesus." He shook his head, looking up at the ceiling. I glanced up to where he was looking

"It's not so bad Darryl. He cares about animals. That's more than I can say for half the little boys his age. I've caught more boys squishing frogs or torturing bugs-"

"That's not it Clare. The kid is skipping school. He's only six years old for Christ sakes! This is the third time this month he's cut out of school. It's always something with him, first I found him in Smith and Wesson's stall, they needed company he said. Then he found a fawn in the swamp. I told him to leave it alone, it was waiting for its mother. Now a badger. You know,

123

I'd understand if this was high school, hell, skipping out to go hunting with his buddies or what not. But he's six!"

"Darryl, Kyle is afraid of you. He says you hate him." I looked at him point blank, waiting.

He just looked sad. Putting his hand to his forehead he started to cry. I looked away.

"What am I supposed to do? Yeah, I might be a little harsh with him sometimes, but I'm so goddamn tired. So goddamn tired." He put his face into his hands.

I stared at him a second feeling uncomfortable, then reached over and gingerly touched his sleeve. "I know you have it hard."

"He misses Dee Dee, that's the problem Without her it just seems like we're unraveling. I need a woman. Kyle needs a mother," He looked at me, bleary eyed. "Not that you would understand Clare."

So now he thought I was cold hearted. "I might not have any kids Darryl, but I see how it could be hard. If you need a break, send Kyle over to my house. I enjoy having him around. I mean that."

He wiped his red face with his hands and looked at me.

"Well," I stood up hurriedly. "I need to get going. I've got a badger in the truck waiting on me."

"No…I'll take care of it," He said slowly. "I'll take it out back, shoot it."

My heart skipped a beat. "Hell if you will. I put a lot of work into that animal. It's coming home with me."

"See ya Clare," He put his face in his hands again.

"Bye." I walked out to the truck, and got in. Mr. Pepper welcomed my return by hissing at me.

"Oh cut it out." I drove the hundred yards or so to the cabin. A car was parked in front I didn't recognize. A nice one. I frowned, wondering which one of Dan's alcoholic buddies would own a Mercedes. Too upscale for White Cloud AA.

"Dan?" I held the cage in front of me as I walked in.

He would get a real kick out of seeing a badger up close. You hardly ever encountered badgers in the wild. I put the cage on the table and threw my coat over the back of a chair.

I heard the squeak of a shutter blowing in the wind. Have to get that fixed, I thought idly. Leafing through the mail on the table I kicked off my boots.

The squeaking continued, getting faster.

I walked directly over to the bedroom door and threw it open. Dan jumped up and grabbed a blanket, quickly wrapping it around himself. The woman lay there propped up on her elbows. A sheet covered her to the waist. I glanced at her breasts and then up at her face, recognizing her as someone I had seen from Moe's. Neda was her name, Neda Pierre.

"Privacy would be nice here." She stared me down as I motioned for Dan to come out of the bedroom.

"Damn it Clare, what in the hell do you want?" Dan shut the door behind him. He stood there staring at me wrapped in a pink and green quilt.

"That isn't very Christian Dan," I hissed. "And just what the hell are you doing?"

"Being a Christian doesn't mean not having sex, or saying a few well-placed damnits once in a while."

Neda came out, tying her thin leather coat at the waist.

"Bye Dan. Call you later. Sorry to intrude on your space Clare." She gave me a sideways glance as she quickly breezed past us.

The screen door banged behind her.

"So now what? Are you jealous?" Dan looked at me inquisitively.

"Jealous! First of all I wouldn't have a relationship with someone like *that*." I grabbed my coat off the back of the chair, hanging it in the closet

"What's wrong with Neda? We enjoy each other's company."

"Oh I'm sure she enjoys a lot of men's company."

Dan folded his arms across his chest and looked out the window. "What Neda has done in the past is really not your concern now is it?" He looked over at me, eyes like chipped granite.

"It is if you're my brother and live in my house and think you're going to be having sex all hours of the day!"

"Clare, look, my personal life is mine, and you need to stay out of it. I'm sorry Neda doesn't meet your criteria, but that's the way it is." He kept looking at me.

I avoided his gaze. "I need to eat something and get back to the office." I opened the fridge and scanned the contents; two pieces of American cheese, some eggs and a green pepper.

"Dan, you need to go shopping, you cleaned us out."

"This isn't about shopping, quit trying to change the subject. I'm sick of your avoidance techniques."

"And I'm sick of you trying to climb inside my head. Leave me alone!" I slammed the fridge shut.

"Hey…let's talk. Like the grownups we are." He sat down at the kitchen table, quilt draped around him. "What's this?" The badger was hissing, trying to get as far away from Dan as he could.

"It's a badger." I slumped into the chair next to him. Drumming my fingers on the table, I watched them rise and fall, rise and fall. "You know Dan…" He stared at me expectantly. "There's nothing to say. Just nothing. I don't know what it is."

"Too many challenges, expectations?"

"Not challenges, I'm used to challenges. The expectations…well, yes, I expected someone different then who you are."

"Anything else?"

"Well, maybe," I took a deep breath. The buttons of my uniform stayed tight. Constricting me. I exhaled. "Maybe I've had to adapt to some things here, maybe that's the problem."

Dan hugged his knees, wrapping the quilt tighter around himself. "It's okay you know, we can get mad at each other, not fall apart." He smiled.

"Yeah, I guess," I picked at a stray thread coming out of my pants. "I just want things to be orderly," I sighed. "I don't know what the hell I feel anymore. I haven't had to feel for a long time."

"Yeah I know." Dan stood up and did a shuffle hop to the bedroom.

I cracked up. "You look like a goddamn chicken."

Chapter 20

Pheeny sat at the kitchen table earnestly powdering her nose. They had arrived late last night, throwing themselves onto their respective beds after quickly surveying the cabin. It didn't amount to much, she thought, although it was cute in its own freaky way, if you liked 1960 cabin decor. Orange carpet, wood paneled walls. Landscape paintings that resembled no scenics found in Northern Michigan. They were of palm trees and the ocean.

Cole lay on the couch in front of a blazing fire. He doesn't look like he is going to move any time soon, she thought with irritation. She studied him in her compact mirror. He was wearing blue sweatpants and a Chicago Bulls sweatshirt.

"What's with all the face paint?"

Pheeny snapped her compact shut, avoiding his eyes. "Time for breakfast." she said.

"Yes, breakfast. We could round up some eggs, bacon, and toast, I took the liberty of bringing breakfast food up. It's in the back of my trunk."

"What? In the back of your trunk? You have eggs rolling around back there?"

Cole laughed. "No, their snug in their carton, in a cooler. Have you ever heard of a cooler?"

"Of course I have, goof ball."

Pheeny looked around for her boots, discovering them by the door in the corner.

She was wearing her woolen sweater with the snowflake pattern and brown corduroy pants. It made her feel woodsy.

Pulling her boots on, she faced Cole. "You don't expect me to cook do you?"

"Of course not. Goofball. I brought it up, now I'll cook. I just wondered if you would be so kind to dig the food out of the back of my car? Since you're up and everything." He looked from the fire towards Pheeny, eyes falling on her boots. "What are those on your feet? They look like they have three inch heels." He laughed.

"That would be correct, they are three inches high. Fashionable, yet functional," Pheeny looked down at her feet. "Oh, I get it, you expect me to wear those clod hopper boots around, the kind men wear. Well excuse me, Mr.Outdoors, I do like to dress like a woman. Because I am one. Unless you haven't noticed."

She huffed out the door in exasperation. Fumbling with the keys in her mittened hands, she found the right one and opened the trunk. She pulled the cooler out, groaning with the weight of it. She staggered back a few steps, then steadied herself. Heaving the cooler through the cabin door she glared at Cole.

"All right Potter, I don't know where you get your eggs from, but they weigh a ton."

She opened the cooler, surveying its contents. The cooler contained cheeses, meats, two loaves of bread, and a variety of odds and ends. Pheeny dug deeper down and pulled out a bottle of champagne.

"To celebrate our time off," He said. "Look, I'm sorry, I guess it sounds like I jumped all over you for no apparent reason - first the makeup, then the boots, yes, you are a woman and a very beautiful one at that." He took a deep breath running his hands through his hair. "It just makes me nervous, having you seem so pressed for time, so up and at it already. I want to get into a different rhythm up here, not so much pack everything into an appointment book as fast as we can. I know it can be hard to unwind, but let's just try okay?"

Pheeny turned her back to him, blushing. She put her hand to her neck feeling the heat creep up to her face. Beautiful. Wow. When was the last time someone had called her that? She couldn't remember.

She picked a couple of tomatoes off the bottom of the cooler. "How would you like an Italian omelet? I see you have all the ingredients here." She turned to face him, tossing a tomato from hand to hand.

"I thought you didn't want to cook?" Cole eyed her doubtfully.

"Well, I thought I'd be nice and cook you up something you probably haven't had before. But I don't want you to get any ideas, you know how men can be."

"How can men be?"

"Expecting the woman to cook, attend to all the domestic chores, that sort of thing."

"No, I never thought that, and never will. My father skipped out on us when I was a wee lad of five. It was just my mom, my sister and I. And guess what? I got to do a lot, I mean a lot, of cooking," He sat up on the couch and folded his arms across his chest. "I believe in equality between the sexes, and I didn't come here to play house and quibble with you."

Pheeny launched the tomato at his head, and Cole caught it deftly in his left hand. Grinning, he tossed it back to her where it rolled across the table and onto the floor. Pheeny picked it up and brushed it off, surveying the damage. The nerve of this guy, she thought. Still, he was kind of funny.

Smiling, she started to chop the tomato.

"My dad used to expect my mom to cook. He was pretty traditional, typical old world Italian. But he always told me to go as far as I could go professionally. That I was really smart and should make something of my mind," She continued chopping, thinking of papa. "You know," Pheeny lay down the knife. "I never thought of it quite like this, not until our little spat…oh forget it." She picked up the knife and started chopping the onion.

"Tell me."

"All right. Well, I think it was, is, confusing for me. What is a woman's role, what can she be?"

"What about what *you* can be?"

"Yeah right. Anyway, on one hand he expected my mother to be passive and submit to him, and on the other hand he didn't want me to submit to anyone. It's almost like there was no one good enough for me, maybe like I was his own special pet?" She looked at him quizzically, then tossed some butter in the pan, watching it melt as she turned the pan from side to side, coating it.

"So what does your mom think of your being a high powered prosecutor and all."

"Oh mama, she wants me to be happy, but her big thing is relationships. She wants me to get married."

"And you don't want to?"

"No."

"Oh."

Pheeny concentrated on cooking, Cole on the fire. She felt like an idiot for telling him so much. Who knows what she'd tell him next, maybe that she was wearing red satin underwear. She smiled to herself. It made her feel sexy.

"Equality huh?"

"Equality."

"Fine. Than you get to do the dishes."

"That's okay by me."

Pheeny put the omelets on two plates, passing one to Cole. She then broke apart the French bread, buttering the pieces well. Cole took a mouthful of egg.

"Mmm," He closed his eyes in appreciation. "Just perfect. I might have to marry you." Winking, he gave her a sly smile.

"Not likely. My mother would drive you insane. Do you know any old world Italians?"

"Yeah, you."

Pheeny had a thought so outrageous, she burst out laughing. "Why don't you come home with me for the Christmas holidays? See for yourself. You can work on your assignments there."

"You're on Ms. Delmato. If this omelet is a small inkling of what I can expect from a Christmas spread at your mothers, I know I'm in for ecstasy."

Pheeny laughed. Mama was going to unroll the red carpet for this guy. She could hardly wait to tell her he was just a friend.

Chapter 21

Joe sat at his desk thumbing through his paperwork, wondering what to focus on. A week ago he had gotten a call from an irate woman whose dry-cleaning business lay on the edge of town. It seems the deer had taken a liking to some chemical in the clothes that had been tossed in the dumpster. They appeared nightly to nibble. Could he please get rid of these deer? He had laughed. Then.

Yesterday it had been one hundred fifty geese on a lawn north of the city. Yes, it was one hundred fifty, I counted them all himself, the man said. He had seemed proud of this. Joe had patiently explained that he needed to let the vegetation grow next to the water, then the geese wouldn't climb up on his lawn to munch on the nice green grass.

The man was adamantly against this idea.

"The place will look like a jungle!"

"Sir, what would you like me to do then?" Joe had felt his patience slip away.

"Get rid of the damn geese that's what!"

Where did these people expect these animals to go? More and more people, less and less land.

People lived in a vacuum where nothing touched them but comforting lies.

The sun came out from behind a cloud, illuminating the room.

He pushed himself away from his desk, stretched, then got up and walked out the door and down the hall, coming to a saunter close to the drinking fountain. The hall was quiet, barren, just like the building.

It was ten to five. Everyone had gone home.

He took a long slow drink from the fountain, the metallic taste sliding down his throat. The faint sound of footsteps came from behind.

"Hey Delmato." Joe recognized the voice, Miles Vandermeen, from down the hall. Miles worked for Geological Survey as a biologist. He had wanted to get in with the Fish and Wildlife Service which he viewed as a proper place for a biologist. They wouldn't hire him. He was still pissed.

"Miles." Joe stood up wiping his mouth. So much for thinking he had the building to himself.

"I hear you're up for the big promotion. Good going guy," Miles mock punched him on the shoulder. "Now you can hire me and get me out of this rock hole."

Joe happened to think highly of Geological Survey, the biologists really knew their rocks. But not Miles.

He scratched his chin, feeling the stubble of five o'clock shadow coming in. "Well Miles, if I did get this position, I'd have to put you on something low profile at first, like the urban deer problem."

"I'm there buddy! Get me rolling and pretty soon I'll be on black footed ferrets, cougars or condors." His eyes were getting bigger and bigger, sexy species obviously mattered a lot to Miles.

Joe yawned. "It's not all that it's cracked up to be, the same old bureaucratic bullshit anywhere you go in government. File this, file that, dot this i and cross this t. The passion goes out of it, pretty soon you become a drone."

His mind started wandering, he had a sudden urge to pick up his camera and fly off to the Amazon.

Miles was frowning. "Yeah well, I'm surrounded by a bunch of old fossils babbling on about igneous and metamorphic rocks all day. I'm going nuts."

Joe studied him. Miles was a nice enough guy, but he was just one guy among many who was trying to get ahead. Trying to play the government scene like everyone else. Wasn't he doing the same thing?

"Hey let's go and have a beer, enough with the shop talk. Save it for the day when you actually get the job."

He considered. But realized that once they got to the bar that's all they would talk about.

"Nah, not today. I'm working my way through these documents. I'll catch you after the holidays though."

"All right then, catch you later. Boss." Miles grinned at him and walked away, hands stuffed in his pockets.

Boss. That little word was packed with meaning.

He walked back to his office, closing the door quietly behind him. The sun had gone behind a cloud again, and the mountain of paperwork wasn't any smaller.

Sitting down, he propped his feet up on the desk and rubbed the back of his neck. His eyes traveled the gray Chicago skyline while his mind wandered among tall birches, moss covered logs, and the deep smells of spring.

Then there was the problem of Pheeny. He had picked up the phone to hear her joyful exclamation that she was in the U.P. She wanted to know what sights to see, what things to do-that sort of thing. Then the bomb had dropped, she was taking a date to the Christmas gathering. Well not exactly a date, she conceded. He was her partner, a business associate. A friend.

Mama's scrutiny would of course turn to him, clucking out her admonitions concerning his lack of a date. Always the mother hen fussing over her chicks.

His mind wandered again to a snow covered woods, to Clare.

He decided then that he would call her.

Chapter 22

Pheeny carefully applied the red lipstick, rubbed her lips together, then carefully blotted them with a piece of toilet paper. She peered into the mirror for the full effect.

Cole, amused, sat watching. "I see this is a daily ritual with you. And what, pray tell, kind of look are we going for today? Little Las Vegas? Mafia queen?" He started laughing, then threw a pillow at her.

"Hey! Watch the face Potter." Stepping back, she surveyed her outfit; black jeans, noir blouse, black boots. She picked a brush up from the dresser and began to vigorously run it through her hair. "Seriously now, I feel like a detective. Don't you?"

"No."

"I'm sorry to hear that. You need to get in the mood, or else we won't find out anything."

"Maybe that works for you, but I don't need to pretend I'm in the middle of a James Bond flick to get information. I'm a journalist."

"Hmm." Pheeney looked over at him, brush in hand. She put the brush down and sat next to him.

"This fire is becoming a habit of yours."

"Yeah. I like it."

They stared into the flames.

"I guess it's hard for me to relax when I have this meeting coming up with Durant."

"Yeah?"

"Yeah." She lapsed into silence. "Tomorrow I will relax. Okay?"

"If you say so."

"You don't seem too worried about finding out anything."

"I'm not. We came up here to get information, and if it's here we'll find it. If it's not, we won't. Have faith in the process, nobody can be fool proof forever."

Pheeny bit her fingernail. "But everyone we have talked to up here hasn't heard of Durant. No one."

"He's not from here. Why would anyone have heard of him?"

"Because he has a lot of land up here."

"So. That doesn't mean anyone has automatically heard of him."

"True."

A log collapsed into the fire, releasing a shower of sparks.

"I'm starting to feel the pressure of this upcoming meeting with Durant, if I don't get something to stick to this guy the case will have to be dropped." She stopped and gazed out the window. "All we have is entirely circumstantial. There's the fact that he took out a large sum of money the day after the murder, possibly indicating a contracted killing. And then there's the statement from the woman in his office that he and Dee Dee didn't seem to be getting along for some reason. That's it. But I know I'm right. I just know it." She looked at Cole.

"Thank God for female intuition."

"Yes," Pheeny stood up. She donned her dark shades, checking her appearance in the mirror on the wall. Blowing a kiss to her reflection, she wrapped herself in her leather coat. "C'mon let's go. We've got work to do."

"If you view going to a casino as work. What's with the shades?"

"Appearances, Potter, appearances."

He clapped a hand to his forehead. "Of course, how could I be so stupid?"

***

A long winding drive led up to the casino. Greeting them at the end of the road was a neon eagle, soaring above the building. Pheeny cautiously turned into the parking lot. "Would you get a look at all the RVs here. Appears that ma and pa decided to take a break from the trailer trip and go gamble for a while. I'm not parking next to one of these things, it's a good way to get mugged." She pulled in next to a small sedan.

"We're not in Chicago anymore."

"You can never be too safe."

They got out of the car and headed towards the entrance. Pheeny slipped her glasses into her pocket.

"Decided against playing James Bond?'

"Yeah. I look too sneaky. This place is huge.'"

"It sure is." Cole held the door open for Pheeny.

The pulsing throb of slot machines hit their ears. Lined up in rows, they ran the length of the casino. Pheeny blinked, trying to adjust to the flashing machines.

"Oh yea. This looks like loads of fun." She stood watching the people seated in front of the slots, endlessly pulling the levers.

She then noticed an Ojibway girl watching them.

The girl was dressed in a black suit and white tuxedo shirt. Her long, dark hair glistened as she walked over to where they stood.

"Can I help you with something?" She smiled.

Pheeny critically appraised her. "Well yes, you wouldn't happen to know Wilfred Durant would you?" Pheeny stood surveying the room, pretending to look for Durant.

The girl followed her gaze. "You mean Willy?"

Pheeny nodded her head.

"Oh sure, he's here a lot. But not tonight," She looked around, turned towards Pheeny. "Would you like to leave him a message?"

"Well sure…tell him Charlene Larue says hi. Oh, and my husband, Clarence." Pheeny nodded towards Cole. "We just feel so terrible about, well, you know, his girlfriend. He's gone through an awful lot." Pheeny dug her nails into her palm.

"Yeah, that is just horrible, isn't it? Dee Dee was a really nice person, I liked her a lot. Her and Willy liked to come up and play black jack." The girl looked over at a beefy blond man approaching.

"Can I help you folks with something?" He looked them over, suspicious.

"Oh no, thank you," Pheeny looked at the girl's name tag. "Lily here has been very helpful. Thanks Lily." Pheeny nodded, found Cole's hand and led him to a deserted section of slot machines.

"Holy shit Potter. Can you believe it? I am so damn good!" She pounded a slot machine in jubilation.

"You are pretty crafty. I have to admit I would never have thought of that approach."

Pheeny noticed that the big blond guy was arguing with Lily. Every once in while he would glance over at her and Cole. "Would you look at that guy, what's his problem?"

Cole turned towards the slots, dropping in a quarter. "Something pretty fishy going on. I think we're on to something."

"Why would Durant take Dee Dee up here to gamble?"

"It's out of the way, nobody is going to talk way up here. He can have a secret secluded life."

"So now we have a link that places them up here as a couple. Now what?"

The beefy blond man stood looking at them, speaking into a walkie-talkie. Lily appeared to have again taken her station as hostess.

"One thing is apparent," Pheeny said looking at the blond man. "We've caused a stir here amongst the security personnel."

Pheeny dropped a quarter in the machine and pulled the lever. The bar leveled at one, two, and then three cherries. As lights flashed and bells dinged a barrage of quarters erupted from the machine.

"Shit Potter! Am I lucky or what?" Pheeny laughed, putting her hands under the falling quarters, trying to catch as many as she could.

Cole watched as the blond man gave them a final look, then turned and disappeared down a dark corridor.

Chapter 23

Dan dipped his brush into a shade of dark green and turned towards the canvas. The scene was of a horse galloping through a meadow, and he began to paint some bushes in the foreground.

"The dipping of the brush into the paint and running it over the canvas is a very sensuous experience." He stepped back and cocked his head to one side, admiring his work. "It's rather like lavishing a lover with the gifts of the divine."

The women in the audience giggled. I rolled my eyes, having had enough of my brother as a sexual creature for one day.

Dan looked out at the audience. "I'm serious. Painting is a very sensual experience. Let yourself feel it with your whole body and soul. Let yourself slip into the dreamy reverie of all possibilities." Dan turned toward the canvas and started painting again.

Everyone bent over their notebooks and started scribbling while the woman next to me glanced over. "You don't have a notebook?"

"Nah. I live with the teacher."

"Ooh." She raised her eyebrows at me.

"He's my brother."

"Oh," She set her eyebrows back down and smiled at me. "Well you must feel lucky having such a talented brother. I think the whole town feels lucky to have him here. It lends a touch of culture to White Cloud. Don't you think?"

"Mmm, I guess so. I suppose I haven't really thought about it."

"Oh believe me, it gets so boring up here in the winter. What are you going to do besides ice fish and snowmobile? The men seem to be content with that," She sniffed in apparent disgust. "So what do you do? Something artistic?"

"I'm the chief wildlife biologist and conservation officer up here."

"Oh. And what do you do with that? Is that like a park ranger?" She bent back over her notes, obviously bored.

"No, it's kind of complicated." I said no more and she seemed relieved the conversation had ended. I was obviously amongst the sordid crew of ice-fishermen and snowmobilers.

Dan seemed ready to wrap it up.

"Okay class, that's it for the week. Next week we'll start nudes. Any questions?"

A woman in back timidly raised her hand. Dan nodded towards her.

"With a real person?"

"Yes, with a real person. Traditionally artists use female models because it is felt that the female body is much more fluid and graceful."

More giggles from the audience.

People began to pack up their things and drift out the door. Some hung around to ask Dan questions concerning their paintings. He would patiently talk to each person explaining concepts of form and color. Encouraging, he had something positive to say about each work.

He looked over at me when the last of the aspiring artists had cleared out.

"Well?"

"Well what?"

"What did you think?"

"What did I think? I think you're asking for a big old gossip session in this town for the next ten years or more if you're going to be using a real nude model. Who do you plan on using anyway?"

"Neda."

"Now why didn't I realize that?"

"C'mon Clare. Be real. What did you think of my instruction?"

I hesitated for a second. "You did a great job. I was impressed."

"You didn't think it was over kill when I went directly from color into form and movement?" He looked at me eagerly, like a dog waiting for a bone.

"Now how would I know that? I'm not an artist."

"You should know now. You sat in on my class."

I sat in my chair and looked around the room. Dan had taken an old warehouse and made it into a studio and classroom. He had found out through Moe that the town council was willing to lease the building on a monthly basis. The whole thing had happened rather suddenly. He was still in shock.

I waved my arm around the room. "Dan, look at all of this, your dream has come true."

He gazed around, lost in thought. "Yeah, it has, hasn't it? And best thing about it is I'm growing roots, getting connected with the community. And my family." He smiled.

"Yeah, I guess I'm family." I stood up brushing off my pants. The place was covered in dust.

Darla walked in from the side door, looking around in wonder. "Hey Dan, this is great! I forgot all about this old building. What did they used to put in here anyway?"

"I'm not sure. Maybe the town's maintenance stuff. There's a bunch of tools in the back room."

"Oh yeah, now I remember. Hey Clare."

I sat back down.

"Clare, where's your drawing pad?"

"I didn't bring one."

"Oh. Well I must be early then. Good, I can get one of the best seats in the house." She sat next to me and started to set up her easel.

"I'm afraid you missed the class." I said.

"Oh no. Gosh Dan, I'm sorry," Darla pushed her glasses up on her nose, giving Dan a pained look. "I told my mom that clock in the kitchen was slow."

"Don't worry about it. Why don't you come over for dinner tonight? I have a little surprise going." Dan put the rest of his brushes away in the old wooden box he kept them in. I vaguely remember my mother using it for something. Probably her pints of vodka.

"That would be great. I haven't been over in a while. That is if it's okay with you Clare?"

"Would you cut it out? I'm just glad you're talking to me again."

She put her hands behind her head. "Well I talked it over with my grandma, she always gives the best advice. She said I should leave you alone. Quit picking at you."

"You *were* picking at me."

"See you at home." Dan saluted us and walked out the door.

She sighed. "Yeah I know Clare, I wasn't being fair. I was just trying to figure out if you really cared for the land."

"Of course I care about the land!"

"But do you feel it?"

I looked away, shaking my head. "Here we go again, I don't want to talk about this anymore."

She picked her pony tail off her shoulder, nervously twisting it around her hand. "Clare, people have been talking-oh forget it, you don't want to talk about it."

"No! I want to know what people are saying behind my back. I won't forget about it." I crossed my arms indignantly.

"All right. Clare, the fishing issue is getting out of hand. People wonder what you're going to do about it. It seems like you don't care, or that you're looking the other way."

"What fishing issue?"

"The Tribe's! There are people out there who are harassing our fishermen. You haven't done anything about it. You need to make it stop Clare."

"What do you want me to do? It isn't within my jurisdiction, I can't enforce the Tribe's treaty rights."

"You can make damn well sure these idiots harassing our fishermen get a ticket!"

"Darla," I said quietly. "I'm sorry. There's not much I can do. I can patrol hunters and anglers on state land, but I can't be everywhere at once. Why don't you tell me of the problem areas, and I'll patrol them more frequently."

She regarded me a moment. "I'll do you one better, let's have a natural resource meeting that includes everything, the bear problem, the fishing issue-everything. C'mon let's get going, we can start right now." She stood up, impassioned by her new educational cause.

"Wait, wait, wait, hold your horses. I don't know. The whole thing sounds very touchy. It sounds way out of my league."

"Clare, you just have to. Quit hiding behind the paperwork dos and don'ts. You need to do what's right."

"Why is this right?"

"Because it will clear the air, people around here will have a better understanding of what's going on with the Tribe's treaty rights."

"So that's what we're after? Understanding?. But what if people don't care?"

Darla started for the door.. "That's a whole different issue. But at least we can say we started the process. Now let's go. I'm hungry."

I followed her, vaguely feeling like I was going from the frying pan into the fire.

***

The phone was ringing when we walked in the door. Dan, Kyle and Harvey were all sitting round the kitchen table playing cards.

"Hallelujah Clare!"

"Hey Harvey. Hallelujah. I've got it,". I grabbed the phone, almost tripping on the badger cage. "Hello?"

"Clare?"

"Yes."

"Hi, this is Joe Delmato. How are you doing?"

"Fine." My heart started pounding. "How are you doing?"

"Great. Mmm, well, I wondered if you would like to come over for the Christmas holiday? It's an annual party my family has, a crazy Italian thing, but a lot of fun. I really want to see you again."

I didn't say anything.

"Clare?"

"We haven't even dated and you want me to meet your family? I don't know, I mean there's my brother here."

"Bring him too."

"I guess you really do want to see me again."

147

"Yeah Clare, I do." The warmth in his voice melted me.

"Let me talk to Dan about it and I'll let you know."

"Talk to Dan about what?" Dan looked up from the card game.

"Just a minute Joe," I covered the phone with my hand. "Joe Delmato wants to know if we want to go to Chicago for Christmas."

"Who's Joe Delmato?"

"Fish and Wildlife Service guy." said Darla.

"Ahh," Dan raised his eyebrows. "Nah, you go Clare, I'm staying home with these guys."

I returned to the phone. "Well Joe…I guess I'll go."

"Great, let me get back with you on the details. I'm sorry I can't talk longer; I'm swamped, but I'll call you soon."

"Okay."

"Bye."

"Bye." I hung up the phone feeling disgruntled. "I can't believe I just did that."

"What?" Dan asked.

"I'm going to Chicago for Christmas. I hardly know this guy."

"Hallelujah!"

"Harvey! You can't do that," Kyle grabbed the cards Harvey had laid down. "Dan, Harvey is mixing up his hearts and diamonds again."

"It's not a big deal, we'll work on it. Maybe we should play an easier game," He looked over at me. "Clare, you like this guy or what?"

"Yeah she does, in a major way."

"I do have a mouth Darla. Yeah, I'm interested ," I sat down next to Dan. "The relationship will never work out though. He lives in Chicago, I live here. There's no way."

"Why do you need everything planned out? Go for it." said Darla.

"Yeah. Live in the moment. Forget the marriage, mortgage, and two point two kids." Dan added.

"All right already. But what about having a Christmas together? I thought that would be nice."

"We can have a little party and open our presents before you leave. Besides, you need your space. I know I need mine."

I folded my napkin into a football, moving it with my finger around the table.

"I suppose your right Dan. We do need our own space, and the two of us living together has definitely been an adjustment."

"Yeah it has," Dan tossed his cards down. "Kyle, you won this hand again, you're getting too good."

I nudged the football across the table, trying to get it to hang over the edge. Harvey snatched it up, examined it, then intently started unraveling it. I wondered what he was looking for. I watched him a moment. His face was an ashy gray, and his hair was wild and greasy.

"Harvey doesn't look so good you guys. Where has he been staying?"

Darla shrugged. "I don't know. I get the feeling he's been wandering around, maybe sleeping in old buildings and barns. Of course he won't tell us where he's been. I was thinking of taking him home with me, but he kind of puts everyone off with his Jesus ranting and raving. Last time I brought him home grandma threw him out. I think he was shoving a cross in her face."

"Holy Jesus Clare, the end!"

"I think he should stay here for a while," Dan said.

"No Dan, that's where I put my foot down," I frowned at him. "I'm not going to get in the habit of taking in every stray that comes in here. I already have a badger that I've got to deal with. By the way Kyle, we need to take him out to the shed so he won't get habituated to humans."

"Clare, he's a human being, not an animal. It's time he started living like one." Dan said softly.

"Of course he should."

I looked over at Harvey again. He and Kyle were silently hitting the football across the table.

Chapter 24

Pheeny glanced at her watch again. Realizing that only two minutes had elapsed since she had last checked the time, she unclasped the watch and dropped it into her bag. Sighing, she started tapping her toe against the tiled floor.

There was nothing worse than getting to an important meeting right on time. She had gotten here a half hour early to go over her notes and prepare herself for this meeting.

But now the anxiety had set in.

Pheeny thought of Cole, and the time that they had spent in the U.P. together. She now wished they had spent more time relaxing.

Her eyes darted to the doorknob as it turned. The door opened and Al Skipton walked in, Durant's attorney. Durant followed behind. She was alarmed to note that Durant was wearing a brightly colored paisley neck tie. Probably an indication of his cocky assurance, she thought. The bastard.

"Very cute, Miss Delmato," Durant remarked, seating himself. "I see you have been questioning my whereabouts in White Cloud."

"Will, I'll handle this. Just stick to the questions." Skipton ruffled his papers out neatly in front of him.

"That's correct Mr. Durant. And I see you have been keeping up on *my* whereabouts. Obviously I must seem like a threat to you."

Durant eyed her coolly. "You're no threat to me. I just know what you've been up to."

"All right," Skipton interjected. "Let's get down to business. Delmato, what have you got?"

"The state has evidence linking the suspect with the deceased in the aforementioned area. Suspect has denied any involvement with the deceased outside of work. So what I want to know Mr. Durant, is what you were doing in White Cloud, Michigan, in a casino, approximately two weeks before her murder?"

"Deidre's spirits were down, so I decided to do something impulsive, something fun. It worked. She had fun." Durant straightened his tie and caught sight of the clock on the wall.

"Anything else?" Skipton asked.

"Impulse?" Pheeny drummed her fingers on the table. "Did you also kill her on an impulse? Are you that kind of man Durant? Because I think you are."

"Ms Delmato, if you're going to harass my client, we're leaving." Skipton stood up.

"All right, all right—sorry about that one. I'll keep my questioning in line. But I need to know why you didn't tell investigators this information before."

Al Skipton leaned over and whispered something in Durant's ear.

"This information had nothing to do with the case, so why would I volunteer it?" Durant smirked at her.

"Did you have sex with her?"

Skipton shook his head. "Don't answer that."

"No. I did not"

"You mean you flew all the way to the Upper Peninsula of Michigan without a sexual encounter with this woman? I find that hard to believe."

"I'm just that kind of guy." Durant smiled, but his eyes remained frozen. "I like to keep my relationships with women private. Surely you can understand a need for privacy Miss Delmato?"

"Will, you need to be careful here." Skipton touched his shirtsleeve.

"I understand privacy Mr. Durant, but a need for secrecy may mean you're intentionally hiding something. Especially if you're a murder suspect."

"Yes, privacy is nice Miss Delmato. Especially if you have been spotted with a male reporter on a number of occasions. And it seems to have gone way beyond the interview stage. If you know what I mean."

Pheeny blushed. "Are you trying to blackmail me Durant?"

"Reporter? Who's that?" Skipton eyed her quizzically.

"Some left wing type of fellow. He likes to cover the radical issues—gay rights, women's rights, you name it. Cole Potter. Isn't that his name? Someone you wouldn't want your name associated with if you were planning on running for public office anytime in the near future." Durant flashed her a hollow grin.

Pheeny stared at him.

"I think I've heard of him," Skipton placed his papers in his briefcase. "We're done here. Anything else Ms. Delmato? Time seems to be running out on this case. I suppose it will be wrapped up in another month or two?"

"Not if I can help it." Pheeny cleared her throat and looked down at her notes. She felt a huge headache coming on.

"Good day Ms. Delmato, and good luck on your crime fighting endeavors." Durant stood up and stuck out his hand.

Pheeny stared at his hand, and then up at his face, feeling a sudden urge to spit at him. She placed her papers back in the folder. Durant withdrew his hand.

"Call me if you have anything new, but from the looks of it this case should be closed shortly."

"Yeah." Pheeny remained seated as Skipton and Durant walked out the door.

Durant swung the door behind him and briefly caught her eye, his face registering smug self-confidence. The door clicked tightly shut.

Pheeny put her head on the table and began to cry.

Chapter 25

Joe had finally called with the directions to his mother's house in Chicago. I had promptly taken out a map and planned my route, estimating it would take me a good ten to twelve hours from White Cloud. I should have tacked on a few more hours.

I was running late and feeling road weary and irritable. Just the state of mind I didn't want to be in when meeting new people. The encroaching twilight made it difficult to see, and I bent over the steering wheel squinting up at the street signs.

A car pulled behind me and honked, then whizzed past. The woman in the passenger seat flipped me off.

I decided to stop and ask directions at the next gas station when the little corner store with the pizza sign appeared. Turning left I breathed a sigh of relief.. I was heading in the right direction.

Five eighteen on eleventh street proved to be a modest brick house spilling over with lights and people. The doorbell had barely chimed when a well-dressed, dark haired woman flung it open.

"Clare!" Grabbing my arm she ushered me in.

"Uh, hello. I'm sorry, but who are you?"

"You mean you don't know? I'm Josephine! I'm sure Joe has mentioned me,. we are pretty close."

She took my coat in the foyer and hung it in the closet. Beyond the entrance there were dozens of people milling around, talking and laughing. The air was filled with the smell of smoke and food.

I was feeling overwhelmed as Josephine again took my arm and led me to the table.

"Sit down, sit down. Let me pour you a glass of wine. You get comfy and relax. .You must be tired from all that driving. Where exactly are you from again? I'm sure Joe told me, but I forgot." She put the wine glass in front of me and I picked it up.

"White Cloud, Michigan." I sipped the wine. It was a warm, rich red that started to tingle me right away.

She looked shocked. "You have got to be kidding me! I was just there investigating a case. Where is he." She looked around frantically for whom I hoped was Joe.

"Cole! Come here!" She frantically waved her hand, catching the eye of a blond man engaged in conversation with an older woman in a low cut blouse. He walked over.

"Josephine, really. I can't believe you left me alone with your Aunt Regine. I think she was getting ready to proposition me."

"Oh I'm sure she was. Clare here is from White Cloud." She nodded towards me.

"Clare, from White Cloud. Wow. You've come a long way. You haven't found Joe in this mess?" He glanced at the groups of people clustered around talking.

"No, but I'm hoping he'll be here soon," I said weakly. The wine was going right to my head.

"Clare, you don't know how fantastic this is! I have been dying to go again since Cole and I got back, but I've just been too busy. You wouldn't happen to know someone named Wilfred Durant or Dee Dee Banks?" She eyed me like a hawk.

"Josephine, will you get this woman some food? She looks exhausted. You can continue your probing after Clare gets some food in her stomach."

Josephine looked at me sheepishly. "I'm sorry Clare, I tend to get carried away." She patted my arm and got up from the table.

Cole took a seat next to me. "You'll have to forgive Josephine, this case has totally consumed her. If she sees the least little lead, she'll pounce on it."

"What case is that?"

"A murder case involving a woman named Deirdre Banks. I'm afraid she has a personal vendetta against one of the suspects, and she's letting it eat her up inside," Cole poured himself some wine from the flask on the table. "I'm sure you must have read about it in the paper."

"No, I haven't, but I remember Joe saying something about it. It's kind of a coincidence, but I live next to some people with the last name of Banks. Well, actually Darryl, he's my landlord, and Kyle, his little boy."

Josephine returned with a heaping plate full of food. Cole was grinning as she sat the plate down in front of me. I dived in unceremoniously.

"What are you grinning for Potter? Did you hear something funny? You look like the cat that swallowed the mouse."

"Funny? Yeah, I guess you could say funny in an odd kind of way. A very funny coincidental kind of way."

Josephine frowned at him. "What are you talking about? Stop it with your silly journalese. Clare, do you like stuffed shells? I made those."

I nodded, my mouth full of food.

"She knows Dee Dee's ex-husband. In fact she lives with him."

Josephine screamed. People glanced over, continuing their conversations when they realized no one was on fire.

She frowned again. "Wait a minute, I thought you were interested in my brother, why are you living with Dee Dee's ex-husband?"

I laughed. "He's my landlord. I live in the cabin next to the house."

"Oh," She looked relieved. "Cole, we need to get back over there and talk to him."

"No, bad plan. I don't think the two of us should descend on this guy. He's already talked to the police. Besides, Durant could hang us out to dry. And we definitely don't need any more bad press."

"What do you think Clare? Do you think he'll talk to me?"

I shrugged. "I really don't know, Darryl's a private kind of guy. But I'm sure he would like to see Dee Dee's murder solved."

"What if I told him that I had new evidence? That I could connect a suspect and his ex-wife in White Cloud a few weeks before her murder?"

"I think he'd go for that. But you would have to approach him carefully, don't pounce on him."

Pheeny smiled. "I promise I won't. Would you mind if you introduced us? I'd like to come up there alone. I think approaching him in a person would be better than calling."

"Sure, give me a call after the holidays. We can set something up," I pushed my plate away, stuffed to the gills. "Dinner was excellent."

"Thank you." Josephine smiled at me, and her smile was warm and sincere. I was beginning to like her.

"Hey, there's the man," Cole got up from the table as he spotted Joe walking over. "Here take my seat, I've got to pay my respects to Aunt Regine." He winked at Josephine.

"You better not." Josephine glared at him.

Cole caught my eye, then mouthed the words; 'she likes me,' behind her back. "Getting more wine for us my dear."

Joe took Cole's seat. "How long have you been here?"

"Oh just long enough to get some food and have a few glasses of wine."

"We've been taking care of her since you were nowhere to be found,"

"I had to get out of here, six hours of constant relative mingling is enough to drive me nuts. I went upstairs to relax and must have fell asleep. What time is it?"

"It's late, and it looks like people are starting to leave. Thank God" Pheeny glanced around the room. "I'm gonna go find Cole. See ya Clare." She patted my arm again as she got up from the table.

"I'm so happy you're here. Did you get lost at all?" He lay his hand on mine.

"No, not really. I was a little overwhelmed driving through a big city, it's been a while." I laughed nervously. I had forgotten how blue his eyes were.

"I thought you said you were from Detroit?"

"I haven't been back there for a while. Long story," I yawned. "I think I'm about ready to hit the hay if you don't mind. I'm really tired."

"Oh sure, I'm sorry, I'll show you to your room, but first meet my mother. She's dying to meet you."

Joe led me towards the kitchen. Josephine and another woman were putting away the food. The woman looked like Josephine, except older.

"The food isn't all going to fit in here, we're gonna have to start unloading it on people." Josephine had the refrigerator door open, surveying its contents.

"Ma, I have someone I want you to meet." Joe presented me like I was the star attraction.

Mrs. Delmato turned around. "Oh my, you're here! Let me look at you," She held me at arm's length and inspected me from top to bottom, her gaze settling on my feet.

"Are you Catholic? Those don't look like Catholic shoes."

Josephine burst out laughing. "You can't tell if a person is Catholic by their shoes."

"I can. I have a sixth sense regarding such matters. So, are you?"

"No ma'am, I'm sorry. I'm not." I smiled politely.

She patted my arm. "That's all right. In this stage of the game I can accept that. I have been waiting a long time for grandchildren."

"I think Clare is tired, she wants to go to bed."

"You take her up to the spare room then, Joseph. Did you get enough to eat? I'll make you a big breakfast tomorrow." She beamed at me.

"Oh plenty, I'm stuffed."

"Good, good. You go now," She waved us off. "Josephine and I have much work to do."

Joe retrieved my bag in the corner of the foyer and we trudged up the stairs together. I opened the door to the bedroom and walked in. The smell was musty, but not unpleasant, just warm and homey. Black and white photographs hung on the wall.

"Who are these people?"

Joe nodded to the photograph next to the bed. "That's my mom's mother and father, from Italy. They'll keep you company tonight," He grinned at me. "I think I'll turn in too. The bathroom's down the hall. Maybe we'll run into each other." He winked invitingly.

I smiled, and tried to swallow the lump in my throat.

He shut the door behind him, and I quickly changed into my nightgown. Sitting on the bed I looked up at the photograph of Joe's grandparents, wondering what they would do in a situation like this. They looked serene with their heads tilted towards one another. I was sure they weren't thinking of sex.

A light knock sounded at the door and I cleared my throat. "C'mon in."

He quietly shut the door behind him and sat on the edge of the bed next to me.

"Well?" He looked at me.

I smiled, feeling stupid. Just what in the hell we were going to talk about half dressed, I didn't know.

He touched my hair, then pulled me to him, kissing me deep and long. I felt myself melting as we lay back on the bed. His hand found my breast, and he slowly circled the nipple with his finger.

I began to feel uneasy, pulling his hand away.

"Joe, let's not. It's too soon."

"Too soon?" He lifted his head. "What are you talking about? We both want each other, and I'm as hard as a rock." He put my hand between his legs.

"Yeah, I can see that, but I don't feel right about it." I crossed my arms beneath my head, wondering why he thought his erection was reason enough to have sex with him. "Everything is so rushed with us. I'd like to take the time to get to know you, to develop a friendship first." I looked over at him.

He averted his eyes and stared up at the ceiling. "A long distance relationship is a very difficult thing, I'm not saying it's not possible, but I think we should act on our feelings for each other. Look, I think of you a lot, and I know I want you."

"I'm attracted to you too, but that's not the point. It feels too rushed for me, and I don't want that."

"All right then, I'll see you tomorrow," He got up from the bed. "Goodnight."

He walked out and closed the door behind him. I stared at the door a moment then laughed, catching sight of my face in the mirror over the dresser. I touched my cheek and looked into my eyes.

I was still the same.

Laying down I drifted off to sleep.

***

True to her word Mrs. Delmato served up a huge breakfast. I once again stuffed myself while I was hovered and fussed over, enjoying the attention. Joe sipped his coffee and watched me, strained.

Josephine dropped by and the atmosphere lightened dramatically. She joked and laughed about the relatives while having coffee with us. I begged off staying another day, saying I needed to get back. Joe said nothing and Josephine looked concerned, saying she would call me.

I left after breakfast.

Heading into Wisconsin I stopped at a small shop on the outskirts of a town advertising Leinenkugel beer and cinnamon rolls. I decided on the cinnamon rolls, tossing them on the seat next to me as I got in the truck. Turning the key in the ignition I glanced over at the bag beside me. Why I'd purchase a dozen gooey cinnamon rolls after I had completely stuffed myself at the Delmato's was a mystery. I shook my head, reasoning it must have been the strange visit that drove me to such impulsivity.

Wisconsin rolled by slowly and I turned the radio on trying to make it go by quicker. I sang at the top of my lungs to "Born in the USA," relieved to be with Bruce and out of Chicago. Starting to feel better I rolled the window down, letting the cold air revive me.

Late in the evening I pulled into White Cloud, and my headlights finally curved around the driveway towards the cabin. I parked the truck and turned the lights off, watching the glow of orange light from inside the cabin.

Dan's silhouette passed by the window and I remembered the cinnamon rolls. Smiling, I grabbed the bag and headed inside.

Chapter 26

Darla was sitting on the edge of a table and swinging her legs when I walked into the conference room. I then noticed something I hadn't anticipated, the room was definitely segregated; half of it was brown, the other half; white.

"Hey! Where's the fed guy?" She looked around me.

"We need to talk." I motioned for her to come out in the hall.

"He couldn't come Darla, Joe Delmato said he had more pressing issues." I looked down at my Catholic shoes. They had a scuff mark on the toe.

"More pressing than this! What is wrong with that man? Everyone is ready to go to war here." She crossed her arms and frowned at me.

"He told me to read up on treaty rights, which I did."

"Clare, I was counting on you."

"Look, I don't know what you want from me, but I'm here to do my part, that's all I can do. Don't expect me to heal old wounds. And why is everyone sitting like that?"

"Like what?"

"Like what! Like separated—Indians on one side, white people on the other."

"Oh, that. It's always like that. Why do you think we live on a reservation? Let's just do this thing." She opened the door and stepped inside. I followed behind.

Darla had set up a podium, which I disregarded. Those things were always too formal for me. I lay my papers on the table, and turned to face the audience. It was a crowded room, and most everyone seemed to know everyone else.

"Hello everyone, I'm Clare McElroy, your guest speaker today," I smiled. "I came today to talk mainly about the problem we had earlier regarding a black bear coming into a campground and attacking a girl. I would like to open this up for discussion, and also fill you in on what has happened so far with the bear problem."

"We already know all that." This from Bart Smithey, a man I recognized as being a smart ass deer poacher..

"Well Bart, why don't you reiterate what we all know then."

Bart looked around the room, chewing his tobacco. "Well, we know you saw that fish and wildlife guy, and he made up some report. The DNR ain't been sued, and the bear might or might not have been killed during hunting season. That's that, case closed." Bart gazed at me defiantly.

"That sums it all up pretty well. Does anyone have anything else to add?" I scanned the audience. "I want to stress that this bear is a rarity. Hank and I are going to be monitoring the situation very carefully, especially the campgrounds in the summer. We've also decided to radio collar some males soon, keeping track of their whereabouts. And of course the bear hot line is still operating down at the office."

I decided this wasn't so bad after all.

"I have something to add," someone from the Indian side of the audience spoke up. "It's all the trash they have that's causing the bear problem."

"Yes?" I peered into the audience, trying to identify who had spoken.

"Trash! Look who's calling who trash." Bart glared over at the Indian side.

His group of poaching misfits chuckled. I identified Charlie Vizneau under a green John Deere cap. Ron Hancock sat next to him. There were a few others I didn't know.

"I think we better get to the fishing stuff," Darla said. "Ms. McElroy said she would address any questions regarding fishing regulations, specifically Indian fishing rights."

"If you mean gill net fishing, that's a crock. Those ain't fishing rights. That ain't even fishing *right* if you know what I mean." More chuckles.

"They catch every last damn fish in the lake with those things." Charlie piped in.

"Historically, the Indians have fished with gill nets, and they will continue to do so. It's part of the Tribe's treaty rights." I said.

"Well I don't consider it a right when we have to pay for fishing licenses which pay for fish to be stocked in the lake. And then they catch them all." Ron Hancock folded his arms across his chest.

"Excuse me." an elderly Indian man cleared his throat.

"You have something to say, Mr. Kewaygishik? Darla asked.

"Yeah, I need to say something. Not until the fish and game were running low did the Anishnabeg people have problems with the whites over this. The commercial fishermen took all the fish for the big cities a long time ago, making the white people. angry, even though it was

166

their own fault. Then the game officers came and took everyone's nets, traps, and hides. Everyone blamed us for the lack of fish. Now, the same thing is happening. When it is convenient for white people to say that we have no rights, they will. But we have a right to fish in these waters." He looked over at Bart and his band of poachers.

"Well McElroy," Bart snapped. "It's a crock, and if I see a goddamn gill net in the water I intend to pull it out."

I put my hands on my hips, my right hand absently resting on my gun.

"May I remind you that we exist in a civilized society Mr. Smithey, of which you of course are a member. And in this society we have a system of laws which we abide by. If you choose to break the law by disregarding tribal treaty rights, well, I'll just have to arrest you. In fact, I will much enjoy it, due to your often blatant disregard of the law. Which, I might add, is the real crock." I glared at him.

He glared back at me. "Woman, you're messing with fire."

"Don't try to intimidate me Bart. You may think you run the show, but I'm the one in charge here." I sat down on the edge of the table and smiled at him.

Bart tried to turn it into a staring contest, but he finally stood up and stomped out of the room, knocking a chair down on his way out. His band of followers sulked out after him, grumbling.

"Well everyone," Darla said. "I think that Bart Smithey and his gang represent an extreme in this disagreement, but I'm sure there are still those out there harboring resentment. I really think we need to talk about this, otherwise, if we don't, the hostility and bitterness will grow. And I think Clare has her hands full of the Bart Smitheys of the world."

"That I do." I noticed the two sides were glancing nervously at each other.

"Does anyone have any suggestions?" Darla looked around hopefully.

There was silence in the room. I looked over at Darla, wondering whether to wrap it up.

Someone cleared their throat in the back of the room. "I don't have any suggestions, but I do have another problem I would like to bring up." He spoke quickly in an English accent.

"What's that?" I asked.

"I'd like to know what happened to my peepers."

"Your peepers?"

"Yes, the peepers in my pond. They're gone. Every spring they're there, but this spring they're not. I wanted to know if anyone has perhaps, netted out my peepers." He looked around indignantly.

I started to smile.

"Can you maybe be a little more specific?" Darla asked.

"I think he's talking about frogs. You know, spring peepers?"

Everyone started to laugh.

"No, I don't know what happened to your peepers, but I'd be more than happy to come and look at your pond."

"Oh thank you, thank you so much," he said, looking relieved. "I'm sure we can figure out what happened to my peepers. We just need to look."

***

Mr. Brimley lived a few miles outside of town. I turned onto a dirt road off the main highway and looked at the address I had written down. It was an old farm house;

tall windows, red barn out back. As I drove in swallows flew from the barn hunting for insects. I watched them sail and swoop, picking out bugs in their airborne path, wondering what it would feel like to fly with your mouth open.

I climbed the few steps to the back entrance, watching as Mr. Brimley walked towards the door and opened it.

"Quite a few swallows you have flying out of the barn."

"Oh yes. They do make a mess with their poop."

I nodded, thinking that somehow the word poop didn't jibe with an English accent. He seemed such an anomaly, this little British man in the middle of the U.P.

We walked through the kitchen and into the living room..

"Would you like some tea?" He put a kettle to boil Mr. Brimley looked at me politely.

"Sure."

The house was meticulously done in a mixture of antiques and modern pieces. A Picasso hung over a large overstuffed couch, with a potted palm situated in the corner next to it. The coffee table was some type of glass and black wood contraption. Dan would love it. All of it.

Mr. Brimley brought the tea in on a little tray. He set it on the coffee table.

"I really like your house. Very artsy, yet also comfortable."

"Oh thank you. I'm afraid I don't have many visitors. Not since Clive died." He took a sip of tea.

"Clive?"

"Yes, my housemate," He waved dismissively at his statement. "My lover actually. It's always difficult to classify one's significant other to the hetero population.

What was he to me? Husband, wife? No, something much deeper." He regarded me thoughtfully.

I sat in silence staring into my tea cup, not knowing how to respond to such a blatant statement of feeling.

"I'm sorry," I finally ventured. "Did he die of AIDS?"

"No," he laughed hollowly. "He was hit by a car. Right out on the main highway here actually. He enjoyed walking at night. Taking the town in, so he would say. I accused him of being a peeping Tom."

I politely nodded, wondering how to turn this subject around to the lack of pond peepers.

"Well anyway…White Cloud seems like such a jump for two cultured gentlemen."

His eyes once again took on that inward repose. "Clive and I wanted to marry a small town. We wanted to go somewhere that spoke of coziness and simplicity. A place uncomplicated by tourism and triteness. Someplace spacious, given to imagination," He waved his hand about, as if to include everything. "So we wound up here. It wasn't quite as we expected, though people are friendly enough." He eyed me politely.

"Oh I'm not from here." I said quickly.

"No? No one seems to be from anywhere in this country." Mr. Brimley's eyes began to get misty again.

"I have a hectic day planned, so I guess we should have a look at your pond." I swallowed the last of my tea.

"Yes definitely." Mr. Brimley collected our cups and put them in the kitchen.

I followed behind him through the kitchen and out the back door. The pond was behind the barn, resting on the edge of a rocky outslope. We walked over and stood at its edge. Cattails lined the edges, and water trickled off the rocky outslope into the pond. It was good size too, maybe an acre or more.

"Such a beautiful thing," Mr. Brimley noted despairingly. "It's one of the main reasons we purchased the property."

I nodded absently, squatting down at the edge of the pond. Peering into the water, I noticed the sludgy phytoplankton soup that characterizes a nutrient rich pond. The phytoplankton was eaten by the zooplankton, which in turn was eaten by small aquatic insects and fish, and so forth and so on, continuing up the food chain ladder.

I watched the water, looking for minnows.

Taking a vial out of my coat pocket, I scooped up a sample of water.

"I just don't know what happened. Every year for the past five years, Clive and I have anticipated the peeping of the peepers. This year, nothing," He watched me anxiously. "Do you have any ideas? A heron stops by periodically and fishes, but I really can't believe he would take all the fish."

I smiled reassuringly. "I don't think it was one heron Mr. Brimley."

"Please call me Bernard."

"Okay. Bernard, it wasn't one heron crashing the frog population. It could be any number of things; some sort of bacteria or virus that's going through the frog population, or maybe the fish numbers are increasing, concentrating on the tadpoles for a food source. I just don't know, but I hope by taking these water samples we can get closer to the answer."

I checked around, looking for evidence. The water trickling off the rocky outcrop caught my eye, and I walked over and climbed up the rocks to get another sample. After I screwed the lid on the vial I jumped down and walked over to Mr. Brimley.

"What I'll do is send these out to the lab for chemical analysis. When I get the results I'll give you a call. It shouldn't be more than a few weeks."

"Thank you so much for all this trouble. I'm sure you will figure it out." He stood there with that misty look on his face.

"Good Bye then, talk to you soon."

He touched my sleeve. "Please, please call me as soon as you here of anything. It means the world to me."

I glanced at his hand and then up at his face. Feeling a rush of pity, I patted his hand.

"I'll call you as soon as the results come in." I headed back to the truck.

As I was heading out of the driveway, I caught a glimpse of Mr. Brimley in my rearview mirror. He was standing by the edge of the pond, watching me leave.

Chapter 27

Bending over the sink I flipped my hair over, blow drying the back of my head. Turning the dryer off I examined my reflection. My hair was growing out, framing my face in soft waves.

I padded out into the living room in my slippers, catching the twang of country music through the open window. Darryl's yodel could be heard accompanying the music.

Dan was bent over the kitchen table, writing intently.

"Damn it!" He threw his pen down. "I can't concentrate." He stared at me, putting his hands behind his head.

"What are you doing?" I sat down, popping open a can of Coke.

"Working on a grant for the studio and continuing art education. What are you doing?"

"Sitting here, enjoying my Coke." I smiled serenely.

"I mean what are you doing today?"

"Oh as little as possible. Maybe I'll join Darryl and do some spring cleaning."

"That's what he's doing up there? Sounds like a hoe down to me," He jumped up, grabbed my hand and twirled me around. "Twang, twang, twang, Billy Bob Thornton, yee haw!"

I fell on the couch laughing.

"Word is he's got a hot date tonight." Dan said winking.

"Date? No way! With who?"

"Someone named Myrna Loyne. Can you believe a name like that? Sounds pretty hot to me," He looked at me mischievously. "Twang, twang, twang!"

I burst out laughing again, rolling of the couch onto the floor. My gut hurt.

The phone started ringing. I got up and grabbed it on the second ring.

"Hello?"

"Clare!"

"Yes?"

"It's me, Josephine. I'm in town here wondering if I can stop by to see you?"

"Josephine…Joe's sister. Wow, this is really short notice. Maybe tomorrow? I'm kind of busy today." I glanced over at Dan. He was back at the table, pondering his prospective grant.

Josephine cleared her throat. "I'm really sorry Clare, but I'm kind of working against the clock. If I don't break this case open, it's finished, closed. A guilty man walks. So it's really rather imperative that I talk to your landlord, Darryl Banks."

I looked out the window. Darryl had set the mop outside the door.

"All right Josephine, I said I'd help. I just wish you would have given me more notice."

"I know, I know. I'm really sorry Clare, but it wasn't until Friday night that my boss gave me this ultimatum. Two weeks, that's all he gave me. Nothing new and the case is closed. I just hit the road as soon as I heard. I barely even packed," she paused a second. "Tell ya what, I'll buy you dinner, how's that? It's the least I can do for your trouble."

"Oh don't worry about it. When can I expect you?"

"Now?"

"Now? Like right now?

"Yes."

"Well, sure…I guess. Do you know how to get here?"

"Yeah. Seems everyone knows everyone else in this town. I'm right down the road from you at the Timberline Ridge cabins."

I laughed. "You mean cabins spelled with an e? Why don't you fix the sign on your way out?

Josephine snorted. "Well I most certainly don't want to offend anyone around here. I think I'll keep my squabbles confined to the courtroom. I'll see you in a little bit."

Before I could say goodbye she had hung up the phone. I placed the phone in the receiver and sat down, finishing the rest of my coke.

"That was weird."

"What?" Dan looked up from the table.

"Josephine Delmato called. She's coming over." I frowned.

"What's the problem?"

"I don't want her to come over. I want to relax."

"Isn't she from Chicago? What is she doing here?"

"She's got a murder case to solve. It involves Dee Dee Banks, Darryl's ex-wife. She wants to come over and ask him some questions."

"Murdered?" He looked at me, horrified. "Man, Clare, this is serious stuff. And you don't want her to come over. Don't you care?"

I sighed and lay down on the couch. "Yes, of course I care. I'm just tired, and I want to *relax*."

Dan sat in the chair next to me. "Are you bummed about that Joe guy, that the relationship didn't pan out?" He watched carefully for my reaction, like he was treading on thin ice and might fall through.

"It needs to pan out slowly. Not flash in the pan," I smiled. "Sex, that is."

"Yeah you're right, it's better to be friends first. I've run into some problems in that department."

"Gee…I wonder why." I rolled my eyes.

"Oh now I see that it's time for Clare to get up on her soapbox. I'm outta here," He stood up. "I gotta go to the studio and finish this. Get away from the twang, twang, twang."

"Fine. Just go," I waved my hand in dismissal. "Leave me in peace."

He grabbed his jacket off the back of the chair. "Don't wait up for me. You never know what will emerge in an artist's world." Laughing, he walked out the door.

I turned towards the window, watching the clouds again.

It was going to rain.

Chapter 28

Josephine showed up while I was cleaning the bathroom. I emerged wearing my yellow rubber gloves.

She stood at the door, looking towards the barn.

"Hi."

Startled, she jumped. "Jesus, you scared me. What are you doing, handling chemicals or something?"

I laughed. "Yeah, you could say that. I'm cleaning the bathroom. Come in." I held the door open for her.

She stepped inside, eyeing the place. "Very little but very cute. Oh, I just love your fireplace! Could we have a fire?," She looked at me with glee. "You know it's spring, but still kind of nippy out way up here."

"Sure." I busied myself with the fire, stacking the kindling, then the larger logs.

"I called Darryl up at the house. He wasn't thrilled, but he said we could stop by later."

"Great. Thanks a lot Clare. I didn't expect that he would jump with joy to see me."

"I told him how important it was for you to catch this guy, that he was your first and foremost suspect." I sat back on my heels watching the fire take hold, creeping along the newspaper edges and licking the twigs.

"It *is* important. You can't imagine how important. It has consumed me. It is my life," She shook her head, looking towards the window. "People just don't get it. They don't understand that I've spent the past year eliminating suspects and gathering evidence. They don't understand the feeling behind my hunches, the intuitive knowing. You know…it's justice that guides me. It's what I do." She shrugged, gazing into the fire.

I watched her as she talked and felt her passion. Her drive. I understood, but I felt embarrassed.

"Coffee?"

"That would be great."

I brought out our mugs. She thanked me, then looked at me a moment. "Does your job do that for you?"

I hesitated, thinking of the right answer. "I suppose I care deeply about my job, but I'm just not as expressive as you, or other people I know." I thought of Dan and Darla.

"Hmm," she regarded me with interest. "Any word from Joe?"

"No. Not a peep."

"I told him he was an idiot for not pursuing you more, oh, how should I say…hotly. That's an apt way of putting it."

I blushed thinking of Joe and I in the spare bedroom. "Oh Josephine, it really doesn't matter, we live so far apart."

"Yeah, but I watched you two, you guys are good for each other. So much in common." She shook her head.

What could I say to her? He was her brother

"I think I ruined it, he feels like I'm a cold fish." I blurted, then winced, feeling like an exposed nerve.

"Oh sure, you might be all coolness and reserve on the outside, but on the inside you're a hot tamale," She beamed at me, unconcerned with the emotions my confession had caused me.

I sipped at my coffee while my face turned red.

"Anyway," she said. "Joe wants to quit his job and start in with his photography full time. He's quite good. Did you get a chance to see his stuff?"

"No, he never mentioned it." I gazed out the window. The horses were in the field.

Josephine had gotten up and stood before the fire. The bear carving Fisher had made me caught her eye. She picked it up, turning it over in her hand.

"This is interesting, such fine detail. Where did you get it?"

"A friend of mine carved it. He seemed to think it was my essence."

"A bear?" She studied me, then the carving. "Nah," she finally said. "I don't know what I'd picture you as. I'd have to think about it." She placed the bear back on the mantle. "I wonder what my essence is. What do you think?" She turned around in a slow circle, hands on hips and nose in the air.

"An animal? Hmm," The nose and the penetrating stare were a dead giveaway. "A bird of prey."

"A bird of prey?," she looked confused. "Like what, an owl?"

I laughed. "No, I guess I was thinking more along the lines of a hawk. Or an eagle."

"An eagle," She smoothed her hair. "Yeah, I like that."

I stirred the sugar in my coffee.

"You know, I feel kind of silly mentioning this," I nodded in the direction of the bear on the mantle. "But I usually carry that carving as a kind of talisman or something."

"Really? What for, good luck?"

"Well, Fisher, the guy who made it for me, is kind of a mystical guy. He has a reputation around here as kind of a psychic," I shrugged. "Anyway, I carry it around as a kind of reassurance I guess. Like some people would carry their St. Christopher medals, or wear a cross."

She nodded.

"I don't suppose Joe told you the bear story did he?"

"Oh yeah, that's how you two met."

"Yup. The bear."

"The bear."

We lapsed into silence. Josephine came to sit next to me on the couch. She followed my gaze out the open window.

"Horses! Oh my god, you guys have horses?,"

"Well, yeah. They're Darryl's."

"Let's go look at them, c'mon!"

"If you want we can go riding. It's such a nice day. Why don't we take them down to the beach?"

"You're kidding me." She stared at me unbelieving.

"Of course not," I laughed. "You act as if horses are some kind of weird, exotic animal."

"Clare, I live in Chicago."

I opened the door. "C'mon city girl, let's go."

***

We drove to the head of the beach trail and I parked the truck, looking over at Josephine. She had quizzed me non-stop about horses and riding on the drive over.

"I guess there's nothing more to ask. I just have to do it, huh?"

"Yup."

I opened the trailer door and led Smith and Wesson out. They stood looking at me patiently. Josephine came to stand beside me.

"I can't do this Clare. They're so big."

"Sure you can. Time to conquer your fear."

180

She looked hesitantly at the horses. "You won't ride very far from me will you?"

"No, I'll stay close. I'm going to let you ride Smith, he's pretty mellow. He doesn't mind a stranger riding him as much as Wesson here." I patted Wesson's rump. He turned his head to look at me.

I pulled some sugar cubes out of my pocket. "Here, make friends," I handed a few cubes to Josephine. "Put them in your hand flat like this, so the horse doesn't bite your fingers."

Josephine followed my lead, and fed the sugar to Smith. He nudged her hand for more.

"No more, sorry." She held up her empty hands to Smith. He nuzzled her pocket. She laughed.

"All right, foot in stirrup," I said.

She grasped the horn, put her foot in the stirrup, and hoisted herself into the saddle. Just like a pro, I thought. I quickly mounted Wesson before Josephine realized how high she was and wanted off the horse. Starting Wesson down the trail, I turned to look at her.

"He'll pretty much follow. Remember, if he goes to fast, you feel scared, or you want him to stop, pull back on the reins and say: 'whoa.' You're doing great." She had that worried look on her face again.

The trail was a meandering mix of conifers down to the lake. Every once in a while I'd glance back to check on Josephine. Her face became more relaxed as we went along.

At the end of the trail the trees parted and we headed down to the beach. I let Wesson break into a slow trot because I knew he'd be excited to get down to the water. I turned around to look at Josephine. She was grinning.

The horses reached the water and put their heads down to drink. Wesson quickly drank his fill and started along the water's edge. An old boat house stood about half a mile down the shore. I turned to tell Josephine.

"We'll pass this old boat house, and then go maybe a few miles more."

She nodded.

As we passed the boat house, I heard Josephine behind me. "Hey, horse! Stop! Where are you going?"

I turned to look, Smith was headed up towards the boat house.

"Clare! What's wrong with this horse?"

I went back to where they stood, Smith had stopped in front of the boathouse. He bent his head down and sniffed at the ground. Josephine dismounted.

"I guess he wants a break." She studied the old weathered building.

I pushed on the door. To my surprise it creaked open. It smelled musty and old inside, with an underlying odor of something rotten. We peered in, adjusting our eyes to the darkness. It was empty.

Josephine gasped and grabbed my arm. I followed her gaze to the floor. Lying in the dirt was a human hand.

***

We took the horses home and I had promptly called the police. Sergeant Kepola met us at the boat house to take our statements.

"So you opened the door and there it was. The hand." He looked at us expectantly, pen poised over his notepad.

"Yes, just like we explained, nothing more, nothing less." I said.

Two cars pulled up alongside us. The word 'Forensics' was marked on one of the cars in black, block letters.

"Well, I don't see why we need to chit chat about anything else. You already told me all you know. It's just strange.   Very bizarre." He took his cap off and scratched his head.

"I think it may involve a murder case I'm working on." Josephine said quietly.

"What?" Kepola gave her a puzzled look

"A murder case involving a woman named Dee Dee Banks. I think it may be her hand."

"She was murdered in Chicago wasn't she? That's the last I heard."

"That's the official story."

One of the forensic guys was waving Sergeant Kepola over. "Well ladies, I see I'm being summoned. If there's any other info I need from you I'll give you a call, otherwise you two are free to go."

We watched him walk away from us, then walked back to the truck.

"I don't think we should mention the hand to Darryl." Josephine said looking at me.

"Yeah, me neither." I kept my eyes on the road, imagining what it would be like to know your ex-wife's hand was in a boat house not far from where you lived.

"So you really think you got a fix on the guy who did it? I glanced over at her. She looked out the window.

"Yeah. He's a real psychopath. I've got a few tid bits of his doings in my files, mainly domestic assaults. It seems he keeps beating the shit out of his girlfriends, then hides behind money and power. He's pretty hard to touch. Once I get him I'm finished."

"Finished?"

"Yeah. Done with the case." She closed her eyes and leaned her head back on the seat.

I pulled into the driveway. Kyle was out in the yard playing on the tire swing that was tied to the ancient maple. He came running over.

"When are you going to take me horseback riding?" He demanded.

I felt exposed, like I had been too close to death to be in front of him.

"We'll go soon," I touched his hair, and he leaned his head against me. "Kyle, this is Josephine."

"Hi." He said shyly.

Josephine smiled at him. "Wow, you're a lot bigger than Clare let on. How old are you, nine?"

"Seven," he said proudly, beaming at her. "Are you here to talk about my mom?" He suddenly looked serious, the eyes of an old man.

She bent down to his level. "Yeah. Yeah I am. I want to catch the man who killed her and put him in jail. I need to ask your dad a few questions. Is that okay? Is he here?"

Kyle nodded, running towards the house. We reluctantly followed. Darryl met us at the door.

"This won't take very long Darryl, Josephine just has a few questions."

Darryl's eyes fell on Josephine, down to her chest, then up to her face again. Josephine smiled at him. He kept running his hand through his hair.

"That's okay, I have time. Why don't you two have a seat?," He ushered us over to the kitchen table. "Coffee anyone? Kyle, you go up to your room now."

Kyle stood in the doorway watching us. He quickly turned and left.

"Ah no thanks, I've had my caffeine quota for the day." I sat down.

"Sure, I'll have some," Josephine took the cup in her hands, warming them. "This old house is great. So homey. You and your wife, oh sorry, I should say ex-wife, live here long?"

Darryl sat down opposite Josephine. "We lived here about five years. I inherited the house from my parents. After my mom died Dee Dee and I moved in."

"Did you know any of the men she dated after you were divorced?"

"No, no I didn't," Darryl shifted in his seat, visibly uncomfortable. "Once in a while she'd come back and get the horses to go riding, I thought maybe it was with a boyfriend, but I never asked. The horses were hers, well mainly Smith, I rode Wesson usually."

Josephine and I looked at each other.

"Did you ever go riding on that old beach trail?," I piped in. "You know, the one at the end of Craven pond?"

"Oh yeah, we went down there quite a bit. Dee Dee liked to run that horse along the beach, made her feel free I guess. She was pretty headstrong, independent. She loved it up here, but couldn't live here. This place was too small for her. She needed to roam." He looked at Josephine.

She nodded.

"Did you ever notice that she came into a lot of money before she died. Maybe got expensive presents from a boyfriend?"

Darryl scratched his head. "Yeah, now that you mention it. She drove up here once in a fancy Ford Explorer, brand new. She was wearing some new boots that day too, riding boots. I asked her about the vehicle and she just laughed. I think then it hit me. I knew it was a guy, but I didn't say anything."

Josephine nodded again, sipping her coffee.

"I guess I really don't have anything else. Nothing I'm sure you haven't told the police."

Kyle appeared in the doorway holding a wooden box. He looked at Josephine.

"I have some of my mom's things if you want to look. Maybe they can help."

"Kyle, there's nothing there, just some of your mom's old things. Put it away son and go back to your room. This is grown up talk."

"Oh Darryl, let him show her. He wants to help."

Darryl frowned. "All right."

Kyle sat the box down in front of Josephine. She opened it, extracting a Barbie doll.

"Well known to every American female. Clare, did you play with these? Or let me guess, you played with GI Joe, right?"

I laughed. "I chopped the hair off my Barbie, then took her out rock climbing."

She picked up a pile of letters, leafing through them. At the bottom of the box lay a small book.

"What's this?" She picked it up, opening it.

Darryl shrugged. "I don't know. Never seen it."

"My mom wrote a lot, that was her journal. She was going to be a writer."

Darryl nodded. "That she was. Such dreams that woman had." He sighed.

Josephine caught her breath and handed me the book. I turned to the page she had scanned. The words; 'Willy and I went dancing!,' jumped out at me. I looked over at her and our eyes met. No one had ever known. This little book was a testimony. I handed it back to Josephine.

"Mr. Banks, would you mind if I take this diary with me?"

"No, go right ahead. Anything I can do to help. I owe that much to Dee Dee." He sighed again, then took a sip of coffee.

Chapter 29

Pheeny placed the mug of hot tea on the bedside table. Plumping up the pillows she arranged them into a comfortable nest, then got into bed. The diary lay on the table by the tea. She had been waiting for this moment for hours.

She adjusted the covers around her as Jinkies jumped up to investigate. He swished his tale and stared at her.

"C'mon Jinks." She patted the bed next to her. Jinkies padded the bed with his paws, searching for the perfect spot. Once he found it he curled up next to Pheeny and promptly fell asleep, purring loudly.

She took a sip of tea and flipped towards the end.

Thurs. Sept. 18

Had a royally screwed up day at work. The copy machine broke, and the service man can't come until tomorrow. A million property questions, everything from legal to water perk tests. I felt like throwing the phone against the wall.

Leave it to Willy to really come through for me. He can be so gentle and caring. He told me to take the rest of the day off, Maxine would cover for me. He said he'd tell the office staff that he had sent me out on assignment. They can be so jealous. Maxine gave me the dirtiest look when I left.

Willy told me to get down to the Sheridan spa, that it would all be taken care of. I left so excited, what an adventure! When I got there the masseuse gave me a full rub down for a whole hour. Then I had a facial and my nails done. I have never felt so relaxed.

Then…dessert. I got home and opened the door. A roomful of flowers greeted me. And a trail of rose petals led to the bedroom. There lay Willy; glass of champagne in hand on new satin sheets. Perfect, just perfect.

Pheeny sipped her tea. The ground work was being laid. He certainly was conniving. She turned to the next entry.

Fri. Sept. 26

I don't know what got into Willy. He hit me. After he told me it would never happen again. It did. I told him the night before that he better not clear the land next to the reservation, I loved it up there. I was really mad at him. He told me I'm too damn mouthy and I should mind my own business. Then he just kind of laughed at me.

Then today… Well, if truth be told, I think he was just irritated, that's all. He had a major deal blow through, and was kind of hot under the collar.

Still, it hurt. My eye was black and blue. I did my best with makeup, but I felt like an idiot when Maxine clucked at me and rolled her eyes.

Willy told me he'd take me up north and make it up to me. Play a little black jack, and sit in the hot tub. Sounds good to me.

Pheeny absently flipped through the pages before she started at the beginning. Durant had purchased land by the reservation? That questioned bothered her. The phone rang.

"Hello?"

"Glad your back. Miss your side kick?"

She smiled.

"Yeah. So what's it to ya?"

"How about some late night Chinese?"

"Sounds good. Pick up some wine too. I think we'll have a late night."

He was silent.

"Cole?"

"Yeah. I think I'll bring my tooth brush. Is that okay with you?"

"If you take it with you when you leave."

"Be there in a few."

"Bye," Pheeny hung up the phone. "Jinks, I think we have an overnight guest."

Jinkies opened an eye and peered at Pheeny. Seemingly unconcerned, he stretched, then curled up into a ball and fell back to sleep.

The phone rang again. She snatched it up.

"All right Potter, I know you're excited, but just get here and we'll talk."

The person on the other end of the phone cleared their throat.

"Miss Delmato?"

"Yes? Who is this?"

"I'm sorry to bother you so late ma'am, but I had to call you about some information I have. You know a guy named Little John, right?"

"Yes."

"Well ma'am, I'm a friend of his, or was, I should say. He had some information for you, but they killed him, so now I gotta tell you. It was bugging John real bad."

"Who are you? Who killed him?" Pheeny jumped out of bed and started pacing the floor.

"I can't tell you either of those questions. What I need to tell you is what John needed to tell you. He felt that it was only right, even though it was dangerous. He wasn't the one to kill Dee Dee Banks you know."

"Yeah, I know."

"She was killed because she was going to spill the beans. There was a major development going up right next to the reservation in White Cloud. No one knew about it. It wasn't legal. Dee Dee knew about it, and was going to go tell some people in town she knew, a sheriff and a judge, I think."

"So who killed her then?"

"I think you know that."

"I have my theories, but I want to hear it from you."

"I'll tell you this, my brother was the one to clean up the mess, but he didn't do it."

"You know, I can figure out who you are, and have you subpoenaed. This is serious shit." Pheeny's heart beat so hard she felt it jump into her mouth.

"I know that ma'am, but I wish you wouldn't. This guy has fingers in everyone's pie, and he can easily get to me."

"You mean Wilfred Durant?"

He was silent.

"Well?"

"You bet."

The phone clicked. Whoever it was had hung up.

Chapter 30

I had been surprised to see the red light flashing on the answering machine when I got home. Dan usually cleared the messages right away.

It was Moe telling me to pick up Dan at the tavern. It seems he had had a bit too much to drink. "What could you expect from an alcoholic?" Moe had said. He sounded worried.

As I pulled in, I thought of what I'd say, if anything. It was one of those wild Saturday nights in White Cloud and cars were parked everywhere.

I looked around the room as I walked in and noticed that Dan and Darla were in a booth in the corner. Dan had his legs up on his side of the booth.

"Hi." I slid in next to Darla.

"If it isn't my sister the know it all. How you doin?" He tipped his beer towards me.

Judging by the way he looked and talked he had been here a while.

"I came to give you a ride home."

"Why should I get a ride home from you?," He narrowed his eyes at me. "You're a Hitler."

Darla put her hand on his arm. "Dan, remember what we talked about? Your sister wants to help. She cares about you."

"My ass. All she cares about is being left alone. She don't like me."

"All right Dan, let's go. Thanks for keeping an eye on him Darla, I appreciate it."

"No problem."

Dan just stared at me, making no move to get up. I was getting more irritated with each passing second.

"Are you coming or what?"

"No, I'm having another one."

"I think not." I grabbed the back of his neck and hoisted him out of his seat, marching him out of the bar and into the truck.

"Why did you do it Dan? What's up with you?"

"Nothing. Nothing at all."

"Look, if you're going off the deep end you can pack your bags tonight. I'm not going to put up with this bullshit. Understand?"

He looked at me. "Do you always have to be such a cop? Can't you ever be understanding?"

I got a flash back of when we were little. He was crying outside, and me the big sister comforted him. Some kids had been poking at a dead squirrel with a stick.

"What you're doing is hurting yourself, and I can't allow that. I'm not going to enable you to do that in my home. I'll be there for you if you really want to change; I'm always here to listen. God knows we had a shitty childhood, but if you do this again, I'm going to have to ask you to leave." I gripped the wheel firmly, satisfied with my little speech.

"You're right," He said quietly, looking out the window. "I've been an asshole."

"What happened? I thought everything was okay with you."

"I didn't get the grant for the art studio."

I looked at him. "Because of that you want to throw your life away?"

"Yeah. Yeah, I'm sick of trying. When I found out I went to the studio and started kicking paintings in. I stopped myself when I realized I was being an idiot. Then I went to Moe's."

"He *let* you drink?"

"Of course not," he snapped. "I sat with some friends of mine, and they bought me some beers. Moe found out later when he walked over to our table."

"Some friends."

"Yeah, well." He looked out the window.

We rode in silence, bumping along when I failed to miss the potholes. Headlights flashed in animal eyes. I felt as if we were being watched.

"Well, Dan," I forced a cheery note in my voice, trying to sound optimistic. "You're just going to have to start from scratch, that's all. It can be done. Look how many times you've done it before."

"That's the point, I don't want to do it anymore." He covered his face in his hands.

"It is a cycle you can break, you don't have to keep doing this. You build yourself up, then tear yourself down, again and again. Just stop, okay?" I parked the car and looked at him.

"I don't know Clare, I just don't know." He looked out at all the stars in the night sky. I looked too.

"It's going to get cold tonight. Freezing. Everyone's flowers, kaput. C'mon let's go in."

We walked inside and I threw my keys on the table.

"I'm going to bed." said Dan

"All right, see ya in the morning."

I sat down on the couch and looked at the fireplace. The gray empty space made me feel lonely, cold. I went over and added newspaper and kindling, then struck a match and lit the edges of the paper. They quickly caught, whipping into a blaze. The heat felt good and I lay down and pulled the afghan over me.

***

I awoke with a start to the sound of birds chirping. Pale morning light shone through the window. Yawning, I turned over, the fireplace was cold and bare again.

I lay back listening.

"Dan?" The empty house echoed my reply. I got up and looked around; Dan was nowhere to be found.

It was then I heard the sound of chanting. It sounded like it was coming from out by the barn. I walked outside, heading towards the noise. A movement in the grass caught my attention. It was Harvey, kneeling over something.

"Harvey? Are you okay?" I walked over to him and he looked up at me, then down again.

I then saw what he was praying over, hidden in the grass. It was Dan. Eyes fastened on the sky.

***

The next few days passed in a haze. I didn't know the first thing about planning a funeral. Does anybody? Moe said he would take care of all the arrangements. He told me to just get through the week; that was all I had to do. I was grateful he took over.

I was strangely removed from it all, like I was watching myself from afar. People said that I was handling the tragedy really well. I would smile halfheartedly, not feeling a thing.

Then there was the question of who to tell. Of course once word got out I was receiving sympathy cards and casseroles galore. Everyone liked Dan. But what about my father? Did he care? I finally broke down and called him. He said he had a business trip and couldn't make it. A business trip? Somehow I wasn't surprised.

I'm in a fog, I told myself. Just like Dan was.

I bought a black dress and started wearing it all the time. This apparently aggravated Darla.

"Clare, I'm worried about you. Why don't you wear something different? Everyone knows you're in mourning."

"Doesn't everyone mourn in their own way?," I picked a casserole off the counter. "Here, stick this in the oven. I got a bunch of people out there I gotta feed."

I felt a sense of duty. I was used to that. Tidy it up, put it away. Even Dan's body could be handled this way.

A hollow sensation began to overtake me. But instead of worrying over this lack of feeling I felt relieved, spared.

A few days after the funeral I decided to go back to work. There was really nothing left for me to do at home. I had given away most of the leftovers, written all the thank you notes. Putting away my black dress I donned my uniform.

Hank was sitting with his feet propped up on the desk when I walked in.

"Clare! What are you doing here?"

"Looks like I'm going to work Hank. Do you have a problem with that?"

"No," he stammered. "But your brother just died."

"And now he's buried."

I walked over to my desk and sorted through my mail. A letter from A&L laboratory caught my eye and I quickly tore it open, scanning the report.

"This is insane. The lab says the water sample has enough DDT in it to kill an elephant," I stared at the report, disbelieving.

"Yeah, I know," Hank looked uneasy. "There's another message for you, the boss called. He wants you to call him."

"Any particular reason?"

He shrugged and bent over some papers on his desk. I watched him as I quickly called headquarters in Marquette.

"Louis Merril please."

"Speaking."

"Since when do you answer your own phone?"

"Since my secretary went on vacation and forgot to hire a temp."

"I heard you wanted to talk to me."

He cleared his throat. "What's this I hear about you getting soft over the Indians? I've been getting hit over the head with calls from people complaining about you. They say you won't let them hunt or fish on so called Indian land, that you've been confiscating guns or fishing gear if they're caught harassing Indians. C'mon Clare, what is this? You know better than that."

"Lou, I'm doing my job, enforcing treaty rights. That's what I'm doing." I felt my face turn red.

"Treaty rights! What the hell is that? That's not your job, you work for the state, remember that. Remember who you're loyal to."

I was silent.

"And another thing, these test results you got back from A&L laboratory, this is sensitive information. It appears the contamination is coming upstream from some land cleared next to the reservation. I want you to keep this quiet. It seems this involves some of the higher-ups and the man who owns the land, a Mr.Wilfred Durant. We need to keep this away from the press, so do what you can."

He cleared his thoat again, listening for my response.

"I know I can count on you, but I wanted to give you the run down before you heard it from Hank."

The silence was deafening, but I knew when it hit me it would happen all at once. It had to.

"Clare?"

"That is such a crock of shit."

"What?"

"You heard me, I am not going to cover up any environmental contamination, and I *will* enforce Indian treaty rights. I wouldn't be a law enforcement officer if I didn't."

"You won't be anything for very long if you don't do what I ask."

"Well Lou, it looks like you and your old boy network can shove it right up your ass."

"You can't speak to me that way!"

"Yes I can. I quit."

"No you can't, you're fired!"

"Whatever." I hung up the phone.

"Jesus Clare, what happened?" Hank was staring at me wide eyed.

I started laughing. "Oh me and the boss had a little misunderstanding. I quit. And since I won't be working on Mr. Brimley's pond problem anymore, could you give him a ring and tell him he has major DDT contamination?"

I threw the report on Hank's desk and walked out the door.

Chapter 31

Pheeny listened to Skipton's closing arguments with little interest. He had made a good case, but now he was all theatrics. Pheeny saw through him, but she knew the jury didn't. They were chosen for their susceptibility.

He had refuted the evidence bit by bit. The hand, he had said, could possibly point to the murder being committed in the U.P., but it didn't in any way point to his client as being the killer. Witness allegations of a relationship between Dee Dee and Durant were just that, allegations. People would talk, because people liked to talk. It was just gossip. He even went so far as to question the witness's character and sanity for alluding to such things. As for the diary, well that certainly was a woman's misguided fantasy wasn't it?

She felt eyes boring into her. Turning, she caught Durant staring at her, a smile on his face. Pheeny looked away, glad of the fact she wouldn't have to see Durant after today.

She stood up. It was her turn.

She walked over to the jury box, and they looked at her expectantly. She smiled. Today she was wearing her floral tapestry suit with a cameo brooch. She wanted to come across as warm and nurturing, your basic maternal qualities. She did in fact feel like a mother.

Pheeny was wondering what to do about the diary. As always, she played the case by instinct. And as she mentioned the diary as evidence she had a feeling that there was a story to tell, and Dee Dee Banks had to tell it. She wanted the jury to know this dead woman; her hopes, her fears, her relationship expectations. They needed to get a feeling for a real live, flesh and blood woman.

Words could do that.

Pheeny began to read to the jury. She read them key entries which she felt conveyed who Dee Dee Banks really was, and they listened to her with rapt attention. She finished with the last two entries in the diary, the two before she was murdered.

"And that, you see, was the story of Dee Dee Banks."

There wasn't a dry eye among them.

She sat down, feeling exhausted. The case had sucked everything out of her. She looked over at Durant, could tell by his eyes. He knew.

It only took the jury an hour to deliberate, and when they came back it was unanimous.

Chapter 32

It had been brewing in the back of my mind for a while so I went to Fisher's. When I walked out of the woods he was there, sitting in front of the fire. I sat on a stump next to him

"Why didn't you tell me my brother was going to die?"

He regarded me a moment, debating. "What good would that have done?" He blew the shavings off the creature he was whittling.

I stared at him, turning it over in my mind. "I could have saved myself a lot of pain, I could have prepared—"

"Could have tidied things up? Made plans for the big death?"

"Well…yeah."

"Some initiations you can never plan for, you just do. That's the way life is."

"It's not that way for you."

"You're right. It's not."

I stared into the fire. I never would figure this guy out. Never ever.

He held up the carving, an eagle in flight. Every feather, every talon, was perfectly in place. He regarded the eagle with interest. Then, when he was done scrutinizing his work, he threw it into the flames.

"Baptism by fire." He laughed, looking over at me.

"What? Why would you do such a thing?" In shock, I deliberated whether I should pull it out with a stick.

"And what do you expect me to do? Line my walls with these things like a suburban housewife? Get a craft booth?"

He picked up a piece wood from the pile that lay next to him. Regarding it carefully, he turned it around and around. Finally, he started carving.

"Well I still have mine." I took the carved bear from my pocket, turning it over in my hand.

"What are you going to do with that thing? Carry it around to the end of your days?"

"Maybe."

"That bear is long gone you know."

"Really. How do you know? Can you tell me for sure?"

He shrugged. "Throw it in the fire. You won't own it anymore."

"No way. I can't believe you threw such a beautiful thing in the fire. What a waste." I shook my head.

He was silent for a moment, then looked at me. "Your brother was a beautiful thing."

Feeling an ache in my chest, I closed my eyes, willing myself to hold back the pain. I couldn't. Death had beaten me.

I left shortly thereafter, there was nothing left to say.

***

When I got home it had started to rain. What started as a drizzle turned into a deluge. It was if the sky had just opened up and cried.

I lay on my bed and listened to the rain. Delving into the darkness, I didn't even try to swim, but let the emotions wash over me, again and again. I thought of Dan, saw us as little kids; laughing, running through the grass. The sky back then spilled out as blue and infinite as a child's smile.

I awoke once in the middle of the night sweating and screaming. My voice sounded like a terrified little girl.

The hours turned into days, and the days kept revolving; a momentous rhythm. I listened to the phone ring and the answering machine click on. It clicked on until it was full. Then came the knock on the door.

The door opened, and Moe's voice boomed out, "Clare!"

Darla strode right to the bedroom. "Moe, she's in here." She put her hand on my forehead. "She's burning up. Clare, did you take anything? Look at me."

I rolled my head around and tried to focus on her, say something funny. Terror registered in her eyes.

"Moe, look at her!" She grabbed his arm.

Moe sat on the edge of the bed, smoothing the hair off my face.

"Clare?"

"Yeah." I croaked. My voice sounded strange to my ears, I forgot I hadn't used it in a while.

"You're in a bad way. You smell awful and look even worse," He smiled at me. "How long have you here? Darla and I have been calling all week."

I sat up in bed. "I don't know. After I quit my job I guess. What day is it?" I scratched my head. My hair felt like it was coated in oil.

"It's Thursday." said Darla.

"That's a week then."

"Why don't you come home with me?" she said. "You can take a shower, put on some fresh clothes. Eat a good dinner. C'mon Clare, you need someone to take care of you for a while."

I looked at her, uncertain. "My brother's dead."

Darla looked over at Moe again, worried.

"Clare," he said gently. "I think you're having some kind of breakdown. You need to get up and reconnect with people."

I took a deep breath and looked from one to the other. "If you don't mind I'd rather stay here. You're right, I need to get up. This is accomplishing nothing."

Moe studied me a moment. "Well all right. I'll let you get up and around, but I'm coming back tonight to check on you around dinner. So you be ready, because I'm taking you out."

"All right," I conceded. "Is it still raining?"

"It quit about an hour ago." Darla said. She gave me a hug. "We'll leave you alone for a bit. C'mon Moe."

They left, leaving me sitting on the edge of the bed. Sliding my feet into my sandals and hobbling out of the room, I stopped at the screen door, breathing in the fresh soaked earth. The sun was out. I stepped outside, feeling the breeze wash over me. A gleaming on the walk caught my eye, and I looked down. Hundreds of worms lay on the walk; some lay still, drowned in puddles, and some were stranded, writhing about. Pulling themselves through the sodden soil to the driest spot around…they still drowned.

I knelt down and began gingerly plucking the living worms from the walk and placing them in my hand.

Chapter 33

Pheeny sat on the couch looking out the window. She was watching three little girls jumping rope. Thinking of an earlier time, she drifted away. The lace curtains blew gently in the breeze, and the sun shone through the clouds.

People were beginning to stir from the long winter, finally coming out to sit on their stoops and talk to one another as they warmed themselves in the sun.

She was waiting for Cole to come by. After the trial they had grown much closer. More intimate. Pheeny was glad, he was a good friend.

The knock on the door shook her from her daydream.

"C'mon in Potter, it's open."

Joe walked in. "Sorry to disappoint you. It's just me."

"Joe! Where have you been? I haven't seen you in ages."

"I got that promotion, that's why. Busy, busy, busy. And what about you? Word around town is that the top assistant DA is taking a break. Maybe even a permanent one." He sat down next to her.

"Yeah, yeah, yeah," she waved her hand in dismissal. "Do you always believe what the papers say? The truth is I don't know. I need a break. I'm knocked out." She lay back on the couch. "I'm pregnant."

"What?" Joe's jaw dropped. "What are you talking about? You…it's that Cole guy?"

"Yes."

"Are you getting married?"

"No. I don't know. Maybe."

He shook his head, puzzled. "I can't believe you're throwing your career away like this."

"Joe, it's my life. I'm sick and tired of living my life for my career. I need a break. I need perspective." She ran her hand through her hair.

"Have you told mama yet?"

"Yeah, regretfully. But really, what was I going to do, wait until it showed?" She rubbed her stomach.

"Well? What happened?"

"Of course she had a fit. I think she's under the assumption I'm getting married," She watched the girls skip rope a moment. "And what about you? How is Clare?"

"I haven't talked to her in a while. I don't know."

"Her brother died."

"I didn't know that. I should give her a call."

"She's a good person you know." She looked at him reproachfully.

"Yeah. I know."

They lapsed into silence, content with their own thoughts. Outside, a child's laughter filled the air.

Epilogue

I wandered down to the creek and sat down, watching the sun reflect in the current. Beyond the blurb and trickle of the water there was silence.

I don't know how long I sat there. It didn't matter. Darla explained as tribal environmental liaison I was expected to take time out, to feel the connections that ran through everything. I was now on Indian time.

The water flowed, and my thoughts turned inward.

Too much discipline had gotten me nowhere, I needed to learn how to feel again, to ground myself in the earth. Digging my fingers into the dirt I turned my face towards the sun.

The other day Kyle and I let the badger go. It was time. He ran from the cage then suddenly stopped and turned back. He looked at us for a long while and we at him. Finally, he turned and disappeared into the brush. If he was memorizing us in a silent goodbye, we'd never know. But I'd like to think so.

I smiled.

A flicker over the sun caught my attention. An eagle was soaring in the thermals, and as I watched she floated higher and higher, transforming herself into an impossibly small speck in the sky. Then disappeared.

About the Author

Ellen Wilson is a freelance writer/photographer from Michigan. Wilson has worked many jobs before focusing on her freelance career: banding Canada geese; cleaning expensive vacation homes in Northern Michigan; and teaching school kids in England, to name a few.

This is her first novel. Visit Ellen Wilson at www.wilsonswordsandpictures.com.